RECURREN CE

The Morus Series

Book 1

Enjoy! ♡

Lora K. Kroush

PROLOGUE

Two years, seven months, and five days. Still no trace of him.

Of course, I may have had these dreams before this town and my memory fell to decay and corpses, but this is the farthest my brain allows me to recall.

Maybe I knew him in my past life, my pre-disaster life, my pre-curse life. I figure that's the only way I could have prophetic dreams about him every night. Surely, I knew him before this madness, before the infected took over, before my memory was stripped away like the flesh peeling from fevered faces.

Or maybe I've never seen this man in my life. Maybe some*thing* is projecting his gruesome end into my nightmares so I can prevent it.

I've tried to stop his death each night for the last two-and-a-half years. I tried knocking him from the path, jumping to his aid, blocking whatever weapon or disastrous object came his way, and it always ended the same. He has been shot, stabbed, slashed, crushed, decapitated, split open, disemboweled, and suffocated over and over in my mind, no matter how I try to save him.

"Stop trying to save him," my friend Scott advised after my seventh night waking up in a pool of cold sweat and screams.

And I did try that. Once. I stood there and watched as the man's limbs were snapped at sickening angles one by one until the invisible force finally snapped his neck and he fell limply to the dark cement. That was the worst nightmare by far, and I didn't wish to relive it.

I tried to ignore the dreams. That didn't work either. When he would be viciously torn apart in front of me by something unseen, I would try to look away or close my eyes. But some*thing* would hold me in place, so I was forced to watch. No matter how much I fought, I couldn't move and couldn't tear my eyes away from him. It's a special kind of torture, being forced to watch someone die over and over again, even if that person is a complete stranger.

So, I continue to leap blindly to his aid each night, but still can't move.

But I wasn't trying to save him just to save myself the displeasure of watching him be brutally murdered. It's hard to explain. Whoever or *what*ever he is, he has a hold on me. I can't *not* help him.

I decided after the first month that I need to find this stranger. I need answers. I need to warn him. Maybe then all the nightmares will end. My traveling companions agreed to accompany me on this 'mission.' Jacklyn, my best friend, agreed that finding him was one of my only remaining options. Her partner, Emmett, was just along for the ride. Honestly, what could he have better to do in this infected-infested world? Scott wasn't fond of the idea. He doesn't trust outsiders. His only mission in life is to "stay alive," and what better way to do that than to stick together?

So, the four of us have searched. And searched. And searched.

Nothing so far. No sign of him.

With each night, he gets closer to me in the dreams. His face becomes more distinct. He steps closer and closer into the light each night as I slip into the next terror. This makes me hopeful that I am closer to finding him.

Maybe he can tell me what the hell is going on.

Maybe he will know what's wrong with me.

Chapter 1

He comes to me now, as he does every night, strange and immaculate. His hair is a curly golden brown, eyes coffee-bean colored with glimmering caramel centers. He is tan in comparison to myself, but I always look like fragile porcelain. He's only a few inches taller than me, with a muscular build and a relaxed stance. His smile, wide and colorful, allures me, as usual.

Tonight, he is so close I can smell his natural, dirty musk. I can see his chest rise and fall with each breath. This time, I can even hear him speak.

I'm not sure where we are, and I don't care. I listen to him talk. I don't even know what he says. I can't tell if he is speaking another language or if he is just making random sounds. I don't care either way. His voice is smooth and sweet, dripping with honey. Too smooth and alluring to be genuine.

He suddenly disappears, and I'm left alone in the dark. It's not until I can hear his pained scream in the distance that I panic. I strain my ears to listen for the direction of his cry, but it seems to echo all around me.

It almost sounds like he's screaming my name. Did I tell him my name? I don't think so. And yet he knows it, releasing it into the darkness like it's a life preserver, like he is worried for my safety instead of the other way around.

"Where are you?" I yell, my voice shaking with fear. Not fear of the dark. Not fear for myself. It's a new kind of fear, one that I can't force myself to swallow. I run forward, twisting, and turning. Nothing. Nothing but darkness. My chest tightens with anxiety.

"Over here," a new voice calls out. Is someone else here with us? I spin around, and my breath catches in my throat.

The strange man lays at my feet, his arms and legs twisted to impossible degrees, bones protruding through his clothes. His beautiful brown eyes are now clouded with streaks of crimson. He makes a choking noise, undoubtedly gagging on his own blood. His eyes flutter wildly to search for help. When our eyes connect, his widen. He opens his mouth. No sound comes out. Just a stream of blood down the corner of his lip. He reaches for me with a broken arm.

But I can't move.

I watch unwillingly as he sucks in his last breath and dies in front of me.

When whatever is holding me back finally releases me, I pull my hands up to cover my face. I'm greeted by his warm blood on my palms.

"NO!" I scream, flopping to the floor.

Jacklyn turns over on her cot to look down at me. "Are you okay?"

I nod faintly, picking my trembling-self off the floor.

"Same dream?" she asks hesitantly.

I shake my head. "Different. Worse." I can't help but stare at my quivering hands. They are clean and pale now. Good.

Jacklyn gawks at me.

I catch the sweat on my forehead with my arm and rub my eyes. For that short few seconds with my eyes shut, I can still picture the dead man, crumpled on the floor. I gasp and my eyes fly open.

Jacklyn is still looking at me, clearly startled by my nightmare.

"I'm sorry," I say weakly.

"It's okay," she assures me. She climbs out of bed to sit in front of me, folding her legs underneath her body. "Do you want to talk about it?"

"I'm not even sure what happened, to be honest." I speak the words slowly, still trying to shake the image of him from my mind.

"Just tell me what you remember."

So, I tell her about the strange man, as I do most mornings. I give her every detail I recall from my dream. She flits to her dresser to yank out a sketchpad and a pencil.

"Tell me, in detail, what the man looked like," she demands, and sits cross-legged on the floor in front of me.

I do. Relaying his appearance to her makes my cheeks burn. It's embarrassing, dreaming about a stranger. She then asks me to run through the dream one more time. As I explain to her what happened, she begins to draw. Jacklyn is a talented artist. Several of her late-night drawings, inspired by my dreams, are hidden under my mattress. If a doctor pre-disaster had seen these drawings, he or she would want to have our heads examined.

At the end of my explanation, she turns the sketchpad around. Her portrayal of him is perfect, down to the very curve of his cheekbones. Though he looks like a muscular man, every part of his face jumps out at me to shriek *WARNING: FRAGILE*! Perhaps this is because he is on death's waiting list. My head throbs at the sight of his flawless face.

"What do you think that means?" I ask, looking down at my hands again. Still no blood.

"I dunno," she answers truthfully.

"Do you think that when we find him, I might..." I don't finish. The thought of seeing him in real life is almost as frightening as the thought of his blood on my hands...literally and figuratively. But I know it's necessary. I *have* to do something to prevent it.

"No, absolutely not." She lays the picture on the floor, face down. She hesitates before adding, "Maybe it's a warning."

"What kind of warning?"

She shrugs. "Maybe this is your subconscious telling you that you should stop looking for him, or something bad will happen. Not that you'd do anything on purpose, but you know...accidents happen. And if you do stop, chances are he will eventually find you. You know, fate and all that."

I just nod.

"Kaiya, you look really shaken up," she notes.

"I've never seen you react to a dream this way before."

"There's something about him...I can't quite put my finger on it. Something just doesn't feel...right. In the dream, he sounded like he was worried about me, like I was the one in danger. And there was another voice, but I couldn't see anyone else..."

She shakes her strawberry blonde curls until they droop down to frame her face. "Maybe we are meddling in something that should be left alone."

I offer her a quiet "maybe" as I lace on my shoes.

"The guys are already up. Let's get going."

"I'll be down in a sec," I say. I wait until I'm alone to get a closer look of her sketch. I move it to the only window in this third-floor apartment. It definitely isn't one of the better options for a home-base, but it's safest from the infected. The staircase is nonexistent. Must've crumbled, seeing as this was one of the closer towns to the bombing site all those years ago. We can only get to our room through a well-placed bedframe through the hole in the wall on the second floor.

I sit by the window for several long minutes, staring at the drawing, at *him*. I can't help but think about the number of nights I've lost sleep over this idiot. Whatever the hell he did to piss off whoever – or *what*ever – wants him dead, it must be damn bad. I've already prepared a stern scolding for whenever I get to meet this guy. And if I manage to save him in the end, I will deck him. My special *thank you* for the many nights of personal hell.

I sigh, throw the sketchbook under Jacklyn's bed, and look out the window.

Where the hell are you?

Scott thinks he must be in a neighboring county since we have searched for two years with not a single whisper of him. But I know better. Every time we get close to the county's edge, I get this strong feeling, almost like a current pulsing through my arms and legs, like a magnetic field pulling me back to the heart of Caldwell. And then I make everyone turn back.

So, I've never left.

Jacklyn thinks it's some sort of prophetic connection pulling me back to wherever he might be. I think that's a bunch of poppycock, but I guess anything is possible, especially in these times.

Emmett has an even darker view. He thinks the man is infected.

"That's why you're always pulled back," he said once. "You know, the way you can sense the infected…maybe you are drawn to him because he is also infected."

Let me explain.

When we woke up together in the midst of the pandemic, I had a bite mark on my left forearm. Now it's nothing more than a red scar. But I can sense when the infected are nearby. If we are ten yards from an infected, I get a tingling sensation from the bite.

Freaky-deaky, I know. And it makes no sense. Was the tingling from the toxicity of the bite, since the infected were born from radiation?

Think of the infected like intelligent, deformed zombies, except instead of rising from the dead or descending from a viral outbreak, they were poisoned by radiation. World War IV turned to nuclear combat. Bombs were released west of us made of god-knows-what. Bomb omits toxic fumes for several miles, aka a strange radiation. Radiation turned mundane people into crazed infected with swollen brains, extreme rage, and violent tendencies with the craving to kill and/or eat any living thing in their path.

I guess that would somewhat explain my connection to the infected, but does it then follow that the mystery-man from my nightmares is also infected? I don't think so.

Or, at least, I hope not.

"It's about time," Scott scolds me when I find them on the first floor. Jacklyn, Scott, and Emmett stand around what used to be a kitchen table, a tourist map spread on the surface. The top of the crumpled paper reads *Quilt Capital of the World* in big purple letters. Scott has one hand on the map, the other hand holding a red sharpie.

"Sorry." I take my place beside him.

"Another bad one?" Emmett asks, scanning the purple bags under my eyes.

"Same as always."

Jacklyn points to one of the hundreds of X-marks on the map. "Are you sure we've been here?" she asks Scott. "I think I'd remember hitting up a liquor store."

"We cleared it already," Emmett says before Scott gets to answer.

"What about here?" Scott points to a Casey's general store, the gas station beside the bridge over the highway.

"We've already been there," Emmett groans. "We've been everywhere in this fucking county. There is no building unmarked."

The boys strike up the usual complaints. 'We need to go to the city,' 'we need to expand our search,' 'let's stop looking, this is pointless,' 'blah, blah, blah.' Jacklyn argues with them, but I don't pay much attention. I'm scanning the map closely. We have searched every nook and cranny in Kingston and Polo, the outskirts of the county, and even some in the country. Nothing. Today, we have the map of central Hamilton in front of us. We've searched ninety-nine percent of it. But, for some reason, my eyes are continuously pulled to the gas station on the other side of the bridge in town. We've already been there more than once. The last time we checked was about three weeks ago.

"Let's try here," I say, pointing to it on the map.

They shut up.

"Why there?" Scott asks quietly.

I shrug. "Just a hunch."

We walk for about ten minutes, not a cloud in sight. The town is brightly lit by the morning sunrise, but there's no life to it. Nobody. Not even a single infected, though we had well cleared the town of those a long time ago, aside from the occasional straggler rolling in. It's not until we spot the bridge off in the distance that the sky suddenly shifts to grey and sorrowful. The rain comes down all at once, sheets of water bouncing off the pavement to greet our ankles. *Welcome to Missouri*, I think sarcastically as we run down the road, searching through the thick, warm rain for the gas station on the left. The downpour is so thick, in fact, that we can't see the building until we're about eight yards from it.

The station is old and broken down. Most of the pumps have been torn up from the ground, but one remains in front of the store, crooked and severely dented from a possible automotive collision. Cracked lights hang from the awning, wires like a snake curl down toward us. There are two cars, one parked in the grass and one rammed into one of the poles where a

11

pump used to be. Both cars are demolished, broken glass scattered like confetti around them. We'd already searched the vehicles long ago, but they were cleaned out, aside from blood stains on the seats and glass shards on the floorboards. We stand there under the awning for a moment to escape the rain.

We approach the glass door with caution. We've searched this place before, and the door had always been cracked open.

So why was there a shiny new padlock on the door now?

My heart does an awkward flip. Someone's been here. Maybe *he* is here.

Scott curses under his breath. "This lock is impossible."

"Allow me," Emmett says, grabbing a piece of scrap metal from the ground. I jumped in front of the door.

"You don't want to do that," I say.

"Oh?"

"Because we don't know who – or rather, *what* – lives here."

"What makes you think something lives here?" he asks, lowering his dark, thick eyebrows in doubt.

I look pointedly at the destroyed gas pumps and then the door. "Because the brand-new padlock on the door isn't an obvious giveaway?"

"Use your brain, Em," Jacklyn mutters.

"All the more reason to go in," Emmett says. "He could be in there."

"And if it's someone else?" I challenge. "Are we prepared to fight whatever is behind this door? Because that's what will happen when we break in."

"And who's to say that the person – or thing – is even here anymore?"

"It's the fastest way in," Scott agrees.

My instincts tell me something isn't right about this place. Almost like a sixth sense. The erect hairs on my neck make me squirm a little. *Why was I drawn here*? I hesitate before moving away from the door.

"I'm going to try the back," I announce before Emmett starts whacking at the glass with the scrapped steel pipe.

I step back into the rain, pulling my hood over my head as I venture around the side of the station.

The downpour suddenly doesn't feel so warm.

I shiver, glancing around nervously before rounding the corner. The backside of the station and much of the highway has been taken over by overgrown trees, creating a spacious forest. Abandoned trash bins by the back steps are tipped over. Trash is strewn everywhere. Empty cans, beer bottles, chip bags, and shredded plastic decorate the grass like a survivor's piñata explosion, making the backside of the gas station a sort of wasteland. A raccoon, maybe? *Let's not explore the possibilities*. I step around the trash and reach the steps.

My stomach does a little flip; my eyes scan the broken window to the back door. *At least I have a way in*. I have a gut feeling, though, that this isn't going to be good. I pull my hunting knife out of the sheath on my belt and hold it poised at my side, elbow tucked in for a clean strike if necessary.

I reach through the door with my free hand to open it from the inside and step in, careful not to let my feet crunch on the glass. If there *is* someone in here, I'd hate for them to have to come investigate a strange noise. My years of self-training and practice have paid off – I'm as silent as a rodent creeping through the gas station.

The room is dark. I wait for my eyes to adjust, though it doesn't take more than a few seconds. I've always been able to see well in the dark. I prefer the dark. The dark is quiet and calming. However, I hate those rare situations – like the one in my dreams of the beautiful man – where it is so dark that even my well-trained eyes cannot adjust. Pitch black makes me nervous and edgy. I like to know what's coming my way. I need to see what's around me. It is eerily dim in here, but at least I still have an advantage.

It must be a breakroom. There's a giant fridge to my right with memos pinned to the door. The counter along the side of the fridge holds a microwave, a coffee pot, and a toaster oven. A long table remains lopsided in the center.

I stand there for a moment. Nothing. Not a sound, except for the dull thud on the bulletproof glass door out front.

Perhaps no one is here? Maybe. But why lock the place up?

I take a rock from outside the doorway and toss it through the breakroom door. The rock clangs loudly into a rack of expired chips, then skids away. I wait. No sound. No rushing infected or fired weapons. The coast must be clear.

Damn. I was so sure I would find him here. Oh well.

I hold my knife closer and edge towards the doorway opening into the gas station lobby. The doorway leads me behind the check-out counter, where I see and hear Emmett still banging at the lock with the scrap of metal. The padlock breaks free and clangs on the concrete. He reaches to open the door, a triumphant grin spread across his face, but the door doesn't budge. It's locked from the inside. He returns to smacking the glass with the scrap of metal. Jacklyn face-palms behind him.

I scan the room quickly – all clear – and walk around to let the others in. Emmett's face twists into a shocked stare when he sees me inside the store. I open the door, but none of my companions move.

"The back door was unlocked," I explain with a quiet smile. Emmett scowls. He's the first to walk in. Scott and Jacklyn follow.

We all take a minute to scan the shelves. Most of them are bare, as we've raided this place a few times before. The alcohol shelf is mostly untouched, aside from a few bottles of wine we took two years ago. None of us are big drinkers. Scott and Emmett sneak a couple of bottles of god-knows-what into their bags when they think no one is looking. Must be whiskey. Scott likes an occasional shot of the stuff. I can't hardly stomach it. All the canned goods, though, are long gone. There are a couple of chip bags and some candy bars, all of which are expired by over two years.

I decide to explore the gas station a little more as they scan the shelves again. I wander to the restrooms. There's nothing in the guy's rest room, aside from an unflushed toilet with white fuzzy mold growing around the seat. The odor drives me out pretty quick. I spend mongril longer in the lady's room, examining myself in the mirror.

My freckles stand out even more harshly than normal against my skin. I pat my cheeks gently with my hand, but that just gives me a light flush to go with my embarrassing marks. My hair is a little crazy, pulled into an extremely messy – but extremely comfortable – bun on the top of my head. I don't like the way it looks there, exposing all the tiny scars on my neck and collar bone. I twist the hair tie out of my hair and let it fall loosely around my shoulders. That doesn't look any better. I look like I just rolled out of bed. My light brown waves are unruly and tangled, standing out straight from my head in a few weird spots.

I don't know why the lady on the other side of the mirror stares at me like this. I'm not anything interesting, and neither is she. Her green eyes squint at me to mimic my discomfort. I sigh and throw my hair back up. The movement sends a familiar burning sensation down my spine and I cringe. I yank my jacket off and pull down the sleeves on my tank top, turning awkwardly to see my back in the mirror.

It's getting worse, I realize, half-disgusted, half-worried.

The dark, veiny mark that runs along my spine has almost reached my shoulder blades. I first noticed it two days after we woke up in the back of that van. It stung horribly, so Jacklyn looked at it for me. It was only about an inch long then. It grows with each month and occasionally burns or stings if I move wrong. It's darker and longer than before. I wish I could know what it is. I'm scared for my health!

I yank my jacket back on and prepare to leave.

Something reflective on the floor stops me. There's water pooled under one of the stalls. It spills out on the grey tiles in front of the sinks. The water would have dried up by now if it had been there for a long time, so I assume the pool to be fresh. I crouch down, careful not to touch the nasty floor, to peer under the stall.

I'm first greeted with the sight of blood. Not dried blood. *Fresh* blood. Crimson blood. Rusty-smelling blood. It streaks down the side of the toilet, on the inside of the stall walls. A few droplets mix with the water on the floor.

But there's a bigger pool of it closer to the stall door, with something big and fleshy draped in the center.

Then I black out.

Chapter 2

I'm in the dark room again.

And so is he. I only know by the sound of his familiar scream in the distance.

There is only a dim yellow light hanging three feet above my head, so I don't see him until he runs past me in slow motion. His shoulder connects with mine. This is the first time we've ever touched.

I turn to see what he's running from, but there is nothing. Nothing but long-stretching blackness.

He isn't running *from* something; he is running *towards* some*one*.

I look back to see him standing in front of me, a small crystal knife pointed at the mass of people who magically appeared two yards from us. As I look closer, I recognize a certain black-haired woman with a strange new scar running down the side of her cheek.

Mongrils.

Scott and Jacklyn believe the mongrils to be half-diseased by the radiation that drove the infected mad. They're lunatics. We'd seen them a few times and were always careful to avoid them. Once, we were close enough to see them skipping manically through the crumbling streets, gutting infected for sport, talking loudly to each other about how they would magically turn invincible one day and be immune to the infected. That was the same night we saw them kill a loner. The only time we've ever seen another sane human besides ourselves, and they frisked him then slit his throat before we could come to his aid. After that, we've always avoided the mongrils, stayed out sight, that sort of thing. And now they're here, and so close.

He tilts his head back to me. "Go." I can hear his heart racing; it's thrums familiar from the many nights I've listened to it fail.

I don't move. Not only because I'm confused, but because I can't. As per usual, some invisible force has stapled my shoes to the ground.

"Go!" He says again and shoves me backwards.

The moment his hand collides with my shoulder, a burning wave surges through every nerve in my body, and I fall into an unseen black hole.

But not before I witness the black-haired mongril driving the crystal knife into the man's chest.

Even though I know subconsciously this isn't real, that I've somehow been sucked into another lurid nightmare, everything feels devastatingly real. This is the first time he has been tangible.

I can still feel a tingling singe in my arms and legs as I continue to fall deeper and deeper into the dream, farther and farther from him.

****

I'm horrified. More than that, I'm thoroughly repulsed.

Not by my nightmare, but by what awaits me after. I'd hoped the murder scene in the bathroom stall was also nothing more than a dream, but with no such luck. I pick myself off the floor only to see the plasma and flesh are still there.

Normally, gore doesn't bother me. Blood and guts on the floor? Okay, no big deal. I can handle the sight of blood. I can handle seeing someone's insides on the outside of their body. I can handle dismemberment. I can even handle witnessing torture – granted most of this is from my nightmares, and I'm witnessing the torture of a man I've never met, but I imagine the concept wouldn't feel much different to watch in an alert state.

So, the goriness of this situation isn't the issue. It's just some severed limbs, for crying out loud.

Two severed legs, pools of thick blood, some detached toes and fingers, shards of splintered bone sprinkled in the crimson pools, a severed arm…

A severed arm…with my name carved into it.

From the inside of the wrist to the crease in the forearm are the letters K A I Y A, followed by the number 33.

Someone is looking for me.

"How long do you think that's been there?" Jacklyn asks from against the wall.

It has to be recent, since the body parts aren't rotting yet, and the blood is still a fresh red color. "I dunno. A few days at most," I say.

Emmett crouches down next to the crime scene. "No rotted smell," he says, leaning in for a closer look. He pokes at the inscribed arm. Jacklyn gags. He then places his hand in the palm the way a friend takes a friend's hand, sending my stomach into threatening flips. "And still warm." Then dips a finger in the blood.

Nope. That's enough for Jacklyn. She slides to the opposite side of the bathroom and picks a cozy spot between the sinks.

"Everything is warm and fresh," Emmett confirms again, standing. He wipes his finger on Scott's jacket, to which Scott cringes. "This happened *very* recently. Like in the last twenty-four hours recently."

"Never mind that," Scott says impatiently. "Kaiya's name is on an amputated arm!"

"Do you think it's...his?" Emmett nudges me. Jacklyn peaks around the stall at us.

I shake my head. "No." *I hope not.* "I had another nightmare about him when I passed out. If he lost this much blood and were dead, surely I wouldn't keep having dreams about him."

"Well, someone seems to know you," Scott says. He places a reassuring hand on my back, but his touch is in no way soothing.

Scott and I have become close friends in the last two and a half year. Too close if you ask me. He is a wonderful friend. My best friend, in fact, not that I would admit that in front of Jacklyn. But lately, he has become a clingy son-of-a-bitch. I get it. Only four of us, Jacklyn and Emmett are an item, and Scott and I spend a lot of alone time together when they are off doing god-knows-what. And I want to feel something towards Scott. I do. Because he deserves happiness and love, yatta-yatta. But I'm not convinced that is in the cards for me. At least, not for the time being. I feel nothing.

21

"What do you think that number means?"

"Your age?" Emmett suggests with a laugh.

I scowl at him. "Be serious."

"I'm not sure what that means," Scott cuts in. "But you said you had another nightmare when you passed out?"

I nod. "Yeah, though I wouldn't call it a nightmare. More of a…vision, I guess? I've never passed out like that before."

"What made you pass out?" Jacklyn piped up from a few feet away.

"I don't know. I saw the arm with my name slashed in it, got dizzy and queasy and weak all at once, and just blacked out."

"What happened in the vision?"

"The man was there. He was running towards me, and…he *touched* me!" I recall.

"Touched you?" Scott's brows stitch together.

"He bumped into me," I elaborate. Scott's face smooths out. "He was protecting me from mongrils. He told me to go, but I couldn't move. Then he tried to shove me away, and I fell. The mongrils stabbed him." I pause, finding a place on the sticky red floor to focus on as I start again. "When he pushed me, it was like an electric shock transferred from his hand through me. I could still feel it as I was falling." I look up, avoiding Scott's concern, and turn to Jacklyn. "That's the first time he's ever been tangible. What does it mean?"

She shakes her head. "I'm not sure, unless it means that we are close to finding him."

"Or he's close to finding us," Emmett says.

"Maybe we should go," Scott suggests. "If this is fresh, someone's been here, and they might come back."

Emmett nods in agreement and escorts Jacklyn from the room. I take one last look at my bloody name, wondering whose arm this belonged to. I assume the person is dead, given the amount of blood and the missing limbs. Did they die because of me? Because they knew me, or because they were looking for me? Or was someone just using these parts to send me a message, somehow knowing I would stumble upon the aftermath?

"Are you okay?" Scott asks, lingering in the bathroom doorway.

"I have a bad feeling about all this."

"You're the one who wanted to come here."

We decide to walk down the highway for a mile or two, so we don't accidentally lead anyone to our home. The bridge waits for us, but we walk down the exit on the wrong side of the highway – it is the apocalypse, so screw traffic laws. The bridge casts an eerie shadow that threatens to snatch our feet and pull us back to town. With a sinking rock in my gut, we continue forward. Emmett and Jacklyn chatter in whispers a few feet ahead, Scott trailing behind them with me on his tail. The sun sits high above us, giving the asphalt a heated glow.

I continue to stare ahead. Something doesn't feel right. At this moment, I feel like an ant under a magnifying glass. Not because of the heat, but because I feel like I'm walking with a target on my back placed by something out of sight. I stretch my arms overhead and try to casually scan our surroundings. There aren't

23

many places to hide. On one side of the highway lay a barren field of weeds. The other side is swallowed up in widespread trees. I skim the tall branches for signs of life but am only greeted by a couple of birds rustling the leaves as they take flight. Has something startled them? My scar on my wrist tingles, like an itch begging to be scratched.

It's Scott who notices my wondering eyes.

"What is it?" he asks, his question drawing Emmett and Jacklyn's attention to me. They stop walking.

I continue to focus on the unmoving forest as I speak in a low voice.

"We need to move. Now."

"Why? What is it?" Scott steps sideways as if to get a better look at the trees spread in front of us.

"Not sure." I tear my eyes away from the canvas of green and brown. "We are taking the woods."

"If something is in the forest, we probably shouldn't go waltzing into its territory," Emmett says.

"No, Kaiya is right," Jacklyn defends to my surprise. "We are sitting ducks out in the open like this. It'll be

harder for them to track us in the trees."

"But it'll be easier for them to split us up," Emmett glares at Jacklyn, clearly disappointed she agreed with me instead of him.

"We aren't discussing this," I say firmly. "It could be infected, or the psychos from the gas station. I don't want to be on the road when they come through." Scott hurries to my side as we take to the forest, silently saying our fair wells to the direct warmth of the sun. Emmett and Jacklyn follow close behind.

Though being among the trees grants me some relief, almost like a partial camouflage has swarmed us, I still feel that something is about to go down. I lean casually into Scott.

"What is it?" he asks, a bit too loud for my liking.

I try to keep my voice low so he will copy me. I don't break my stride as I murmur. "Have you noticed that the deeper in we go, the scarcer the animals become?"

"No," he says honestly.

"Just keep your eyes peeled. Something is here, and knows we are here."

Scott glances around nervously. "We should go back to the road."

"No. Here, there is a better chance at a fair fight."

"But what about –"

The sound of a snapping twig stops me in my tracks. I throw my hand up to hush Scott. Emmett and Jacklyn stop behind us. The three of them clearly haven't heard the noise. The uneasy confusion on their faces tells me that much. I discreetly point ahead.

It takes every ounce of concentration I have to pick up the sound of breathing and an irregular heartbeat lurking just a few trees ahead of us. But there is something else, too. Something slightly louder and slower paced. It loiters just beyond the first. The sound is familiar, almost as if I have heard it a million times. How can I not remember where I've heard this sound before?

The breathing comes faster, pulling me out of my thoughts. It must be preparing to move. Then the noise multiplies. Whatever it is, there are more close by. I slowly reach for the sheath strapped to my thigh and withdraw a couple of thin – but sharp – throwing knives. I don't look back, only nod forward slightly. I assume the others know to pull out their weapons.

The mongril peaks her head around the tree too fast. I threw my knife, but it just barely scrapped the tree trunk before whizzing to the grass.

An arrow strikes at the tip of my shoe. Then the mongril steps out, and six men follow, guns and arrows pointed at us. We're outnumbered.

"Close," the mongril says, her voice gruff for a woman's. "But not close enough."

Chapter 3

"Who are you?" she asks, slinking forward almost as if she were dancing inebriated. Her voice is sturdy, though, so I doubt there's a drop of alcohol in her system. Must be the radiation, or she *is* partially infected. She is tall and lanky with dark hair and a rectangular face, her eyes dark and bloodshot.

Don't give her your name, my conscience warns.

"Who are *you*?" I retort. "What are you doing out here?"

"Looking for someone," one of her men says behind his gun.

"So are we," Emmett huffs.

"What a coincidence."

The dark-haired woman circles us. Scott tenses behind me, but none of us move. Without looking down, I finger through the throwing knives at my side. I count five. Not enough to take out everyone, but I only need to take out her before they fire. Scott and Emmett have fast reflexes, but would they be fast enough? I decided not to risk it.

When the woman slinkies her way in front of me again, she flashes a toothy smile that doesn't reach her eyes. Her elbow remains arched, arrow staring me between the eyes.

"I'm Blair," she says.

"And I'm the ghost of Christmas past. What do you want?"

"How cheeky! I'm afraid we're going to have to search you."

"And if we don't allow it?" Emmett counters.

"Did I say you get a choice?" Then, over her shoulder, she shouts to her men. "Frisk 'em. If they give you a hard time, show them what we do to noncompliers."

The familiar beating noise from before grows closer.

Before her men can move, something silver flies between Blair and me, sinking deep into the tree beside Jacklyn. It's my throwing knife. I look back at Blair, who dropped her bow the minute the knife soared past her face. It must have nicked her. She has a long, trickling cut across her cheekbone.

What follows is so fast I almost miss it.

Arrows rain down on the six men, leaving two dead and one injured. The dark-haired woman moves to the injured man, the other three joining her. Then an even larger group surrounds us, weapons poised, but not pointed directly in our faces. They wield hand-made spears and bows. And a man steps forward, a man with curly brown hair and sun-dyed skin.

"Are you four okay?" the man asks.

That voice.

He takes another cautious step forward, out of the sun glare and into the shade.

It's *him*.

From my nightmare.

He's exactly as he appeared in my dreams. He looks at each of us, resting for a few seconds on each face. But when he looks at me, his jaw locks. His eyes glint with dread. Does he recognize me? Because I certainly recognize him. But how could he have seen me before?

The scene before us feels like DeJa'Vu. I'm confronted by the mongrils, and the man from my many nights of torture is here – though, he'd never been pointing a weapon at *me* before. This is how my mad, sleepy subconscious had predicted it. This is how it started before he died.

Is this another nightmare? I want to pinch myself, but I can't make my arms cooperate. Just like in my dreams, I'm unable to move. Scott grips my shoulder, confirming that it isn't a dream. His proximity creates a static-like charge, his awkward longing to shield me familiar and hard to ignore. I'm sure he can feel my bewilderment.

I stand there, frozen in my own disbelief, eyes locked with the physical prophecy.

Staring at them.

At him.

And then at nothing.

****

We wake some few hours later in a cold blue room, each of us strapped to chairs seated in a circle. I'm the third to wake. Jacklyn and Emmett whisper intently to one another until I groan about the throbbing in my temples.

"What happened?"

"Dream boy and his Army of Saints shot us with sleeping darts," says Emmett. I snicker at the way he describes them. Jacklyn must have recognized the man from her sketches and filled Emmett in.

"I don't remember seeing the darts," I say. *At least I know I didn't kill him.* I twist my wrists against the binding. Not zip ties. Not rope. Not chains. Some sort of cool, thin metal that carves into my skin the more I struggle. I stop immediately after feeling warm liquid trickle down to my knuckles. Don't want to pop a vein.

"They shot you first from behind. I think they could tell you were leading us," Jacklyn explains.

I nod. "Are you two alright?"

They both nod back to me.

Scott sits directly across the room from me. He's still out. His nostrils appear to be stained with crusted blood, the skin around his nose purpling.

I throw my chin in his direction. "What happened to him?"

Emmett laughs. "They shot you. You went down. Dream boy told his men to hold their fire. Scott ran at him. Dream boy superman-punched Scott. Scott launched at him again, and they opened fire."

I snicker again despite myself. "Silly bastard."

"Why did you freeze?" Jacklyn suddenly asks.

"Why did I freeze when?"

"When you saw him."

"Dream boy," interjects Emmett.

I think back to that moment in the forest, after the knife nicked Blair's cheek and planted itself into the nearest tree.

I don't remember if I felt nervous or panicked when I saw him. He was exactly as I pictured him. Curly golden-brown hair matted to his forehead, strong arms poking out of his fitted red t-shirt, and coffee-caramel eyes staring down at me, causing my knees to lock under my body. He looked stunned, possibly because he had just run into a group of strangers cornered by mongrils. And fragile. His dark aura looked so thin and fragile! Though his clearly defined physique begged to differ.

The only reaction I remember having at that precise moment was swift realization. Over two years of searching, we found him. I can finally warn him. Maybe now, the nightmares will stop. Perhaps they already have. We were clearly knocked out before we were dragged to – well, wherever the hell we are – and I don't recall having any sort of dream.

In fact, I don't remember anything after seeing him. I only remember waking up in the blue room.

Why bring us here? What do they want from us?

When I pull myself back to the moment, I realize Jacklyn and Emmett have fallen silent. They're concentrating on the door.

There are three voices on the other side, only one of which I recognize. I can't make out what the voices are saying to one another, but they sound urgent and rushed. I focus my attention back to the center of the room, where Scott stares me down.

"Are you okay?" I ask. Jacklyn and Emmett are still too focused on the conversation outside of the room to be disturbed by me.

Scott nods curtly and looks away.

I tried to ignore his obvious irritation, but it's difficult. *Butthurt much? Sucks to be outmanned by a stranger, I see.* Oh well. He'll get over it eventually. My thoughts are interrupted by the sound of a key turning in the lock. I brace myself for whomever will greet us.

It's *him*, of course.

He walks in slowly, followed by three armed bodyguards. The guards hang back against the back wall while "dream boy" walks to the center of our musical chairs gathering.

"Hope everyone's feeling alright," his velvet voice penetrates the room. He gives us all a two-second glance, his eyes lingering on mine for a moment. I hope my eyes don't betray me. I try to force myself to glare at him, to give him the nastiest stink-eye I can manage, but once our eyes lock, I find myself flushed with nerves. I'm once again haunted by images of him lying on the ground in a pool of his own blood, my hands stained by his wounds.

I wonder if I've ever made an appearance in his mind, too. If that's even possible. I wonder if he has ever seen my face before meeting me today. I try to read his expression, but it reveals nothing, only cold, unforgiving brown eyes staring back at me with equal intensity. How strange, to see these eyes as cold and unforgiving. In my dreams, they have always been warm and full of spark.

Until they are lifeless and clouded by blood.

"Who are you?" Scott asks the man roughly. Clearly the staring makes him uncomfortable, too. I finally find the will to break eye contact. I glance at Scott with a silent *thank-you* for breaking the long-winded silence.

But the velvet voiced vigilante is analyzing my face. I can practically feel his eyes search me.

Scott speaks again. "Wait, do you know her?"

The man clears his throat, still looking at me.

"You're Kenna, aren't you?"

"It's Kaiya," I correct through thin lips. "Have we met?"

He hesitates. "Sort of…it's a long story."

"Not as long as mine," I say. "And I suppose I don't get to know your name? Before you launch into this *long* story of yours?"

"Dylan."

"Huh."

"What?"

"Nothing. I was expecting some oddball name, like Grayfon or something. But Dylan's pretty normal, as names go."

Dylan stands, then snaps his fingers at the guards. One of them takes a place beside Dylan. I recognize this guard to be one of the men from the forest. He's a bulky fellow with brown hair and a frayed beard.

"Cut her free," he commands.

The guard man obeys. I can't see what he uses to cut the bindings, but my wrists are relieved in a matter of seconds. I rub them gingerly as he frees my ankles. Whatever wounds the metal ties inflicted on me have already healed. Only a tinge of crusty red is left. I don't think much of it at this time. I've been a fast

33

healer as long as I can remember. Once my ankles are free, my wrists are rebound by a zip tie.

The guard scoots over to Scott's chair when Dylan raises a hand at him.

"No, no," he halts. "Just her."

"What?" Scott wiggles in his chair and winces as the bindings cut into his hands. The guard grabs the top of my left arm, his grip rough and tight, then leads me behind Dylan to the door. "Kaiya –"

"It's alright," I call back to them.

But I don't know that for certain.

We close the door behind us, entering a wide, white hallway. Too white. The hall is blinding. Once we are safely into the hallway, Dylan waves the guard forward. The guard speed-walks until I lose sight of him round a corner.

"Sorry about that," he breathes.

"I get it," I say and trudge forward. My legs are stiff from sitting for god-knows how long. "Inflicting fear makes hostages more compliant."

"Not that you're really hostages. It was fun to watch your companion squirm."

"I'm not sure who you mean," I hedge.

We turn a right corner to a short hall. At the end of the hallway are double doors with small, barred windows. Light streams in from the glass, giving the yellow floor two glowing gold squares. I stand in the stream of sunlight, enjoying its warmth as Dylan steps around me to open the doors.

The sun is setting off to the west. Dylan escorts me down the concrete steps to the foot of the oversized garden before us. Once our feet touch the ground, Dylan cut my hands free.

"Not afraid of me attacking you?"

He laughs. "I think I can handle myself."

Yeah, okay.

We walk down an expanding row of carrots and potato plants. Each section of vegetation is divided off by a garden wires, weaved into tiny fences the height of my shin. I glance from one side of the garden to the other. There must be twenty to thirty rows of home-grown food within these protective walls! At the far-right corner against their borders, there's a chain of fences. Two cows in one, about three dozen chickens in another roaming the coop, and six hogs in the last fence.

A couple of people tending to the vast garden stare at me, utter distain coloring their faces as we pass.

"You guys are really...thriving," I say casually. We walk to the far-left side of the garden towards a rundown camper.

"We manage," he says just as casually. Dylan motions me towards the camper.

I enter the rusty yellow mobile home and seat myself at the foldout table's booth. Dylan files in after and sits across from me.

"I have questions I need answered," he says, eyes focused on the table. "And I'm sure you have some for me, as well. But first..." Dylan sighs, and looks up, intensity burning under his lashes. "I have to warn you."

"No. Whatever you have to say can wait. *I* have to warn *you*."

"Huh?"

I continue, ignoring his confusion. "Now this is going to sound strange and impossible. And you don't know me, but I need you to trust me."

He scowls. I wonder what he expects me to say.

He should expect the worse.

Stale air from this overused mobile home invades my airways, but I have trouble exhaling. I've imagined this scenario many times, but it never looked quite like this in my mind.

"I've been having these dreams…more like visions really…for the past two and a half years. You are in them." I stare at him, praying the concern and intensity in my eyes reflects the same in my voice. "And every time I see you in these visions, you…you die."

He's quiet for a moment, brows stitched together in what I assume is confusion. Afraid the silence will grow awkward; I quickly add on to my statement.

"It's crazy, I know –"

"No," he finally speaks, clearing his throat. "It's not crazy."

"So, you believe me?"

"Yeah."

Another pause. Dylan's eyes widen, the coffee centers mirroring his fear, but not the type of fear I imagine it to be. His gulp is visible. He places a hand on the table, reaching across, knuckles turned up.

"I believe you," he continues, "because I've had the same nightmares about you."

Chapter 4

"You've had visions of *me* dying?"

"Every night."

Well, isn't this a fun little twist? My hands involuntarily curl into fists. The camper walls enclose on us, my head swirling my worst fears with concern for my own safety into one knotted ball of yarn, one I can't hope to unravel alone. Sweet hell. And hell's demon, tormented with the task to deliver us both to the burning pits, waiting patiently across from me. Is he even aware of the irony at play here? I wonder if his stomach curls the way mine does now at the sound of his prophesized ending.

"Is that what you were doing out there?" Dylan asks. "You were looking for me?"

I nod, and glance at my feverish hands. No blood. But will there be? Will I be both of our demises? Is that the only way these dreams will end?

"I was looking for a way to stop it," I say through gritted teeth. "But I guess it's kind of pointless now, isn't it?"

"I wouldn't say that. We can stop the nightmares somehow, I'm sure."

"What's the point? We're goners."

"It's not going to happen," Dylan says in a matter-o-fact way.

"What makes you so sure?" I snap.

"I won't let it happen."

"Why? You don't know me."

"It doesn't matter. I saw it, so it's my responsibility to –"

"To what?" I interrupt, slamming my hand on the table. "How are you going to do anything about it if you're dead, too?"

"I don't know" he answers quietly. I make a scoffing noise and stand, turning my back to him so I can gain my composure. After a mute moment, he asks, "Why do you think this is happening?"

"I'm not sure," I admit, still facing away.

"Do you think it has something to do with that Cragen guy?"

I spin on one heal. "Cragen? Who's Cragen?"

The name is foreign to me, but not completely unfamiliar. In one of the dusty corners of my mind, Dylan's voice echoes the name. The crunch of the first two letters ping against my nerve endings. Raised hairs, random twitch. Certain death. Cragen. As if I'm not already on edge.

"You know? Cragen." His right eyebrow pulls up at the corner. "We ran into his group when we found you in the woods."

"Blair? The mongrils?" I ask.

"Who's Blair?"

"Never mind. Just get to the point."

"He makes his people roam the woods in search of survivors. If he finds anyone with morus cells, he pulls them back to his camp where he performs these sick experiments on them."

"Morus cells? Experiments? You're not making any sense."

"You really have no clue?"

"Does it look like I have a fucking clue?!" My eyes sting. I've never handled frustration well. Any sort of anger or chaos makes me tear up. Not because I'm upset, but because I'm using all my strength not to beat sensible answers out of someone. Violent tendencies? No. More like extreme anxiety. I un-balled my fist and flex my fingers. My knuckles still tingle.

"Okay, chill," Dylan points to the poorly cushioned bench. "I'll tell you what I know about him."

I don't want to know anything about *him.* I just want to know why we have nightmares about each other's impending dooms. I want to know how and when I am going to die. Or do I?

I take a seat reluctantly.

"When the radiation of World War IV spread the infection, our government's lead scientists worked on a cure. But there was no cure. So, instead, they created a sort of vaccine. Anyone who has the vaccine can't be hurt by remaining radiation or an infected person's scratch or bite. But before they had the completed vaccine, they had to do some..." he struggles to find the right word. "human testing. Some of the tests went horribly wrong, and people were dying. After several failed tests, they perfected the vial. It was created by something they called 'morus cells.' It wasn't really cells, though. More like an antibody on steroids."

39

"What does this have to do with us or that Craven person?" I demand impatiently.

"I'm getting to that," Dylan says. "So, *Cragen* was one of the doctors from the testing, or something like that. Supposedly before he could get ahold of the injections for his own personal uses, the lab was overrun and burned to ash. He wants to recreate the morus."

"Why?"

"I'm not sure."

"But how does he expect to recreate it?"

Dylan shrugs, his trapezius flexing in a distracting way. Man, he has some wide shoulders. "He's been taking people he finds out there, people he knows have the morus cells. Maybe he thinks he can replicate it if he has a sample." Dylan's eyes squint slightly, frosting over. His every muscle tenses. "It hasn't worked so far. He's taken so many people for these sick experiments. None of them are seen again."

I suppress a shudder.

"That's too bad. I still fail to see what this has to do with what's happening here!" I throw my finger in a circle between us.

"You have quite the temper."

I scowl.

Dylan rolls his eyes. "Maybe the nightmares were part of some sick experiment he did on us."

"I think I'd remember if I'd been experimented on."

"Would you?" he retorts.

Would I? I think back to the day I woke up two and a half years ago. I can't recall many significant events before that day. Perhaps…

But something   forces the thoughts out.

"Well, what about you?" I demand, jabbing my finger across the table again.

"Those mongril people kidnapped me a year ago."

"Oh?"

"Yeah," he says glumly. He pulls up his left sleeve to reveal tiny circular scars running up the inside of his arm. The scars closer to his wrist are silver, but as they extend to the elbow crease, they ombre into a purple, then flatline into a row of grey just above the fold. "They experimented on me for a week. Never saw that Cragen guy, but I heard the mongrils talking about him when they would inject me. I was lucky these were the only marks I received."

I raise an eyebrow at him. "What do you mean?"

An odd expression crosses Dylan's face, one that's gone before I can identify the emotions behind it. "There's a grey line between experimentation and torture, let's just say that."

Every word he's said thus far swims in my ears, but I have no home for these words in my brain. "Look, this is all very confusing. We don't know that any of this is connected to our nightmares."

"Sorry. I didn't mean to overload you with information."

"Maybe we should concentrate less on the why, and more on the *how*," I suggest.

Dylan nods, and his brown eyes grow colder. "Like, how are we going to keep you from dying?"

I chuckle. "I can take care of myself, buster. I'm more worried about how to keep you from doing anything stupid."

"What do you mean?"

I think about my last nightmare, about the knife that pierced Dylan's ribs in a foolish attempt to protect a complete stranger.

Or something stupid like trusting me. I'm still unsure myself, of his prophesized blood on my hands.

Dylan's eyes measure my expression warily.

"I think that it would be best if we didn't leave each other's sides for the time being," I speak the words slowly, emphasizing each syllable to make the importance of both our lives known. "Just to be sure the nightmares don't come true."

Dylan frowns. "I agree, but I don't think that's going to solve anything."

"It's just to buy us some time," I explain. "Maybe we can figure out what's going on, find some magical explanation for it all or some answers from the past, and then we can come up with a plan."

He nods, though the crinkles in his forehead do not smooth out.

"Rylie's not going to like it."

"Who's Rylie?"

"My brother. He doesn't generally like newcomers."

"Well, maybe if we go explain to him –"

"No," he says hastily.

Dylan sighs. No doubt he can see the question on my face.

"My sister had…dreams, sort of like this…"

"…and?"

"She's not here anymore, if that's what you're getting at."

My muscles tense. "So, they're definitely prophetic?"

"I'm scared so."

Silence stales the air between us for an immeasurable moment.

The expression on Dylan's face is unreadable. Admittedly, I wouldn't be able to read his face well anyway, seeing as we don't really know each other. Sure, I've had the same nightmares about him for the last two and a half years, but what is that in the face of his physical presence now, behind the protective walls of his community?

A death sentence. That's what it is.

Perhaps the cold, negative stare he gives the table now isn't everything I chalk it up to be. Maybe it is as simple as fear for his own life. Maybe he is wrapped up in more conspiracy theories about this Cragen fellow's supposed involvement. Maybe he thinks now about his sister and the similar dreams she used to have. This thought makes me wonder what she prophesized in her dreams. What terrors must have lied behind her closed eyes. Did her nightmares conspire to her demise? I don't dare ask. I wonder what she must have looked like. Did she have the same tan skin as her brother? Were her eyes as warm a brown, or her hair as untidy? Did she have the same fragile features as her doomed-to-die comrade?

I clear my throat in an effort to break the silence. "What a grand first meeting, huh?"

"Indeed," Dylan says, his voice hoarse from the silence. "Alright."

"Alright what?"

"Let's go talk to my brother."

****

43

We walk back to the main building in silence, passing a few of the community civilians as Dylan leads the way to a small, dim-lit room with a desk in the corner. Aside from the west wall filled top to bottom with pictures and a lamp on the desk, the room is vacant.

"Hey!" Dylan stops a woman walking down the hall. "Have you seen Rylie?"

"He just stepped out to work on the vehicles, I think," the woman says. She's a petite thing with a blonde pixie cut and short stature. Like most of the people I've passed in this walled village, the woman stares me up and down before moving along with her laundry basket full of garden veggies. Have these people never seen outsiders before? The rude eyes in this place make me want to cover my visible scars.

Instinctively, my hand cups the bite mark on my arm.

"I'm heading that way," she calls over her shoulder. "I'll tell him you're looking for him, Dylan!"

"Thank you!" Dylan hollers back.

I follow Dylan into the room. He stops in front of the wall of pictures, hands on his hips.

"What is this?" I ask him as I browse the oversized collage. So many families of all different sizes and backgrounds reside here, staring back at us. Though the nostalgia is thick, the pictures are nauseating.

"Pictures."

Duh. "But what are they all doing here?"

Dylan rolls his shoulders, eyes fixated on the collage.

"Not all of us were so lucky after the war. My brother Rylie took a picture from our home when the infected took over. With every house we raided, every newcomer we took in, every person we lost over the years, we added a picture." He sighs, face puckered with what I imagine to be grief, though I truthfully do not remember the feeling. He's zeroed in on one specific picture. "But his scrapbook overflowed quickly. We turned this room into a sort of tribute to them."

"Even people you didn't know?"

Dylan looks at me, and I'm hit with more memories of his corpse.

"Everyone deserves to be remembered," he says. He points to the photograph he's focused on with one calloused finger. "That's the picture that started it all."

I scoot closer, ignoring the static between my arm and his, to get a better look.

It's a picture-perfect family. A slim-fit mom with shoulder-length hair, a blue-collar dad with muscles to spare, and three nearly identical children. I recognize, Dylan immediately. His brother, Rylie, is slightly taller with wavier hair and big hazel eyes. The young girl in the middle, I imagine, is their sister. She looks like she stepped straight out of a teen movie. Long, thick, perfectly blown-out silky hair and perfect blue eyes, but her face shape resembles that of her brothers. She is thinner than her siblings, yet still appears athletic.

"My parents died only days after the first wave of infected," Dylan says before I can ask.

"And your sister?"

His jaw clenches. "It happened just as she predicted."

Dread fills the air between us.

If it happened for her, will it happen for him? For me? What is to become of our predictions?

"I'm sorry."

What else am I supposed to say? I don't know him. I can't entirely empathize with him, as I don't recall losing anyone close to me before waking up in that van two and a half years ago – though I had to of lost *someone*, right? Otherwise, where did I come from? Surely, I once had a biological family – but I can sympathize.

"At any rate, it's better this way," he says. "At least she died on her own terms, defending the people she loved. In the face of everything else, I'd say that's a decent way to go."

So, is that why he wants to save me from my fate? To make his sister proud? To die an 'honorable' death, as he believes she did?

"At least you still have your brother," I say in a quiet voice.

And he does. He has someone to live for, someone to miss him, someone to mourn him should the unthinkable happen. Should my prophetic nightmares come to life, Dylan's brother would be left alone.

One of many unexplainable reasons this strangely tangible apparition, straight from the depths of the darkest corners of my mind, *will* not die on my watch.

The door to the room opens, and in floods the silvery hall light, followed by a long-stretched shadow.

"Speaking of my brother…" Dylan says, facing me with a shy smile.

A child-like version of Dylan enters the room, but he doesn't look to his brother. His large eyes are focused on me. I don't realize until now that I am standing in a shadier part of the room. The boy squints, but I refuse to move from the lamp's shadow until Dylan has introduced me.

"Rylie," Dylan announces, moving towards his brother. I am a statue. My feet protest.

The boy, Rylie, is the same height as his brother, but his facial features are not near as mature. His cheeks are rounder, his chin more curved, and his eyes a cooler, gentler appeal. He has a less experienced aura about him, as if life has not handed him quite as many soured lemons as it has his brother. Does he lack in wisdom, or street smarts? By the shortage of warm tints in his aura, I'd say he isn't as awakened to the apocalyptic lifestyle as his older brother. Aside from these subtle differences, the guys could pass as twins.

Rylie continues to study me from afar as Dylan speaks to him in a franticly low voice. I don't have to strain to pick up on his responses.

"You *what*?!" Rylie snaps in a heated whisper as Dylan explains his dreams. His reaction makes me uncomfortable. From the looks of it, Dylan feels the same. He shifts to one leg, lowering his voice even further to apologize for not telling him about the nightmares sooner. I try not to listen in too much as the boys argue about a lack of trust.

I turn back to the photographs, pretending to immerse myself into past lives as they chatter behind me.

"And that's her?" I can feel him gawk at me now. "She looks oddly familiar…"

"Will you just come meet her?" Dylan begs. "We have a lot to explain and discuss."

Rylie sighs. "I guess we do."

The boys shuffle towards me. Rylie's expression is still just as suspicious as it had been when he first saw me. I meet them halfway, stepping to the light omitted from the small desk lamp. Rylie recoils slightly, searching my face for god-knows what.

Before I can blink, Rylie leaps at me, pinning me to the wall with a pocketknife at my throat.

Chapter 5

"What the hell?!" I spit at him.

"Why did he send you here?!" Rylie demands, pushing the knife closer until it touches the base of my neck.

"Who?" I ask, confused.

"Don't play dumb! Cragen! Why did he send you here?"

"I have no idea what you're talking about," I defend. "I don't even know who he is!"

"Rylie, what are you talking about?! Stop it!" Dylan shouts, pulling on his brother's arm.

Rylie shrugs his brother off.

"The desk," he growls at Dylan. "Top drawer to the left. Now."

Dylan throws the drawer open and pulls out a small, rectangular paper. It's a picture. Dylan stares at it for a long second while Rylie stares at *me*.

"I knew you looked familiar." He spits on my shoe.

"What the hell?" Dylan demands to me now. He stomps up behind his brother, holding the picture up so I can see. "What are you doing with Cragen?"

The picture is of a young teenaged boy holding a younger version of me in his arms. We stand in front of a large oak tree with a tire swing. I'm posing for the camera, looking straight ahead, and the blonde boy is smiling down at photographed me.

"*That's* Cragen?" I ask.

"Tell me why he sent you here," Rylie says again, this time drawing the tiniest bit of blood from me. "Now!"

"I don't know who this is! I've never seen him before now."

Dylan glares at me, his eyes hard and cold. "Are you telling the truth?"

"Of course, I'm telling the truth!" I snap.

"Liar," Rylie growls.

"She said she doesn't know. Cut it out."

Rylie turns to look at his brother with disapproval.

A second of distraction is all I need.

I grab Rylie's wrist with my left hand and hit the crease of his elbow with my right. He yelps in surprise and drops the knife. I snatch it just before it hits the ground and point it at them.

They both stare at me in shock.

To show good faith, I close the pocketknife. They continue to stare.

"It's bad luck to close a pocketknife you didn't open." Rylie points at my hand. Dylan rolls his eyes at him.

Bad luck. Aren't we already cursed with such?

"Look," I say, setting the knife down and holding my empty hands up in defense. "I'm not going to hurt anyone. I have no clue who Cragen is, and I don't know why we are in that picture together. All I know is that we are in big trouble here, and we need to get some answers."

"Why should we believe you?" Rylie asks.

I let my arms fall to my sides. "Because if I were here to hurt you, I would have done it already. I'm just here for answers."

"Answers about what?" Rylie asks.

I grow impatient now. "I just want to know why *we* are having these nightmares and how to make them stop."

Rylie turns deliberately to face his brother, a cold burning deep in his gaze. But Dylan avoids the glare, his own eyes pleading me to stop talking.

Rylie's jaw set is audible. Through gnashed teeth, he speaks carefully, eyes still locked on Dylan.

"What do you mean, we?"

Dylan shakes his head.

But I ignore him. "Your brother is having nightmares about my death, just as I have had about him for the last two years."

Dylan sighs.

And Rylie growls again.

"When were you going to tell me?!"

Silence falls over the room.

"Nice to meet you, too."

After an eternity of bickering boys and circular discussions about Dylan's safety (and my own, of course, but I changed that subject every chance I found), Rylie agreed that Scott, Jacklyn, Emmett, and I should stay until we can figure out how to put a stopper on our impending deaths. Each word that Dylan spoke dripped with bitterness. Every time he glared at me sideways, I couldn't help but roll my eyes. Rylie would've found out one way or another.

We talked briefly about Cragen. Very briefly. In those few moments, his name was mentioned, my mind was consumed with questions and impossible scenarios.

How is it possible that I knew Cragen, yet I cannot remember him?

Were we friends? Colleagues? Lovers? We look to be the same age in the photograph, but the joy radiating from the colorful image gives away no hints to the nature of our relationship.

Where did the photo come from?

Rylie said he found it the night he saved Dylan from the mongril's compound, so I know physically where it came from. But where was it before the world ended? Before the infected stormed our cities? Before friendships, relationships, and alliances ended in futile attempts to survive?

Rylie had put the picture back in the desk towards the end of our century-long talk. I swiped it from the drawer and shoved it deep in my pocket before we left the room.

What took me hours to process took the group all night.

Jacklyn and Emmett paced the room, heatedly whispering amongst themselves every few seconds. I stood quietly by the door. No doubt they would have questions for me after their brains processed everything.

Scott stayed seated in his chair – though he wasn't strapped to it any longer – and rubs the purpling spot on his cheek.

When we had entered the room, Rylie cut Scott free first. Scott lunged around him at Dylan. Rylie tried to step in, but Scott shoved him. So, naturally, Dylan sucker-punched Scott. His ego would be wounded for a few days, but he would get over it.

What I couldn't understand in that moment, though, was why it was taking them so long to talk to me. After all, it was my life on the line, not theirs. Why were they so easily heated over it? And why the animosity towards Dylan and Rylie, aside from the obvious reasons?

I told them point-blank that they didn't have to stay.

"*I'm* staying," I had said, "because I *have* to know why I'm having these nightmares. I *have* to stop them if I can because it's the right thing to do. None of you have to stay with me. You can go home or leave town or whatever you choose. I just need to know so I'm not worrying about you guys, too."

Naturally, Scott wasn't going to leave. He switched immediately into defense mode. How dare me not assume he would stay by my side, blah blah blah. I'll spare you the rest.

Emmett and Jacklyn agreed to stay, too, but I couldn't tell if it was out of worry for my safety, new-found trust in our hosts, or simply for safety in numbers. Not that it mattered. I was and am grateful they chose to stay where I am.

Or maybe I'm just grateful that with an axe hanging over my neck, I'm not alone.

****

The next few days behind the walls are brutal, both physically and psychologically.

Rylie and Dylan argue the first night about where we will stay. There are apparently plenty of rooms to accommodate us, but Rylie fears the community will frown upon outsiders under the same roof. After an hour or so of Dylan's warm hospitality and Rylie's frustrated slurs, Jacklyn intervenes.

"It would be nice to be in an open space," she says, glancing sideways at Emmett. "Sleep under the stars, maybe."

So, Dylan finds us a few tents and sleeping bags from a nearby storage room, and we go on an extended camping trip among the crops and livestock. Rylie follows us only to announce that he will be sleeping in the camper a few feet away, no doubt to keep watch over us invaders. Before his brother can argue, he stomps off.

"I'm sorry about Rylie," he apologizes for the millionth time as he pitches my tent for me. I try to explain to him I've done this before, many, many times, but he insists on helping us settle in.

"Don't worry about it," I assure him. After all, the autumn breeze is quite pleasant, as is the open view of the night sky. I could live without the fertilizer smell, though.

"Do you guys always sleep in tents?" he wonders aloud.

"No," Scott answers to my surprise. "We did for the first few months while looking for *you*," a new harshness coats the last word, one I don't recognize from him. Resentment maybe?

"We made a home in an abandoned apartment building," I explain. Then I remember the sketchpad under one of the beds back home and all the crazy drawings it possesses. "We should probably go back for our stuff at some point."

"No need to worry about that now," says Dylan, still assembling the tent in the dirt. "Besides, don't want to have a run-in with the mongrils at night."

"I think we can handle them," Emmett grins.

"Don't underestimate them."

With the tent all but welded to the ground, Dylan bids us a goodnight.

Another night passes. We stay outside, where we receive strange looks from the community people. We are like ants under a magnifying glass, except our perceivers are more disgusted by our presence than anything.

Since we have nothing to do, we train. And boy, do we get some death-stares and black eyes! In a brief practice sequence, we keep close to our tents, I beat Jacklyn and Scott two-to-zero. Emmett and I tie one-to-one.

Dylan comes by our area a few times a day to 'check on us.' Emmett invites him to join the fun as we spar, but he refuses, analyzing the purple ring around

Jacklyn's left eye. He excuses himself to check on Rylie's progress in the infirmary lab. Rylie takes care of the ill and injured while learning the practice of medicine. Not that we would know, as he won't let us in the main building to observe or assist, but we hear quite a bit of bickering from the brothers over Rylie's involvement in the lab.

I mention to Dylan again on the second night that we need to go back for our personal belongings, to which he asks me to wait another day so he can accompany us. *He* wants to 'accompany' *us*! Not like he knows about my built-in infected sensor. Perhaps if he did, he wouldn't bother. Or if he did know, he might go on another silly tangent about his experimentation theory.

The next morning, I wake before the others. I exit the tent I share with Scott – he seems just as weirded out by the arrangement as I am – to find people tending to the crops and livestock. More curious and judgmental eyes flicker to me as I stretch beside my tent. I can practically feel the stares bore into my back as I bend over my water canteen. When I turn around, though, they try to be inconspicuous. One middle-aged woman scolds her son quietly for looking in my direction too long.

I recognize the woman feeding the pigs. She's the basket woman Dylan caught in the hall by the picture room. I don't recall catching her name, but her glower feels all too familiar.

With a deep sigh, I stroll over to her.

"Hello," I say in the politest voice I can manage.

She looks up through her blonde bangs but remains mute.

"I'm Kaiya," I continue, waiting patiently for a reply.

She finally caves. "Yuna."

Yuna. Her voice is golden silk in comparison to my own. Doesn't quite match the maturity in her cheekbones.

"Nice to meet you, Yuna. Any chance I could lend a hand?"

Yuna straightens her back to look me dead on. "You want to help?" Confusion thickens her voice. This new tone sounds more natural with her features.

I nod. "If I'm going to be here a while, I think I should contribute something."

"Uh, okay." Yuna grabs a bucket of slop and hands it to me. The goop sloshes over to splat my shoe. "Dump this in the other trough. I'll finish this one."

Yuna doesn't talk much as we work. I ask her what to do, she tells me how to do it, then we move on to the next task. Sounds mind-numbing, I know, but it beats sitting around the tent, bored, while people silently gauge you.

Scott wakes up and watches me cautiously from the tent.

Yuna's more observant than I expect. "I don't think your boyfriend approves of you helping out."

"Best friend, not boyfriend," I grumble as I plop more radishes in a basket. "He's not much of a team player, to be honest."

"Then why are you all here?"

"Looking for someone."

"And have you found this someone?"

"Sort of."

"What does that mean?"

I sigh. "I think so, but I'm not sure what to do now."

Yuna glances around us. Everyone else is heading to the building with the day's proceeds. The midmorning sun splits through strands of her pixie cut as she crouches beside me, her voice low and saccharine.

"I can dig up some dirt on the person, if you'd like."

I raise a suspicious eyebrow at her. "You'd help me? Why?"

She shrugs with a smile. "You helped me, now I can help you."

I peep around her small frame to see Dylan walking towards us from the camper, his brother tailing close behind.

"I'll help you every day I'm here if you can tell me about Dylan and his obnoxious brother."

"Dylan?" She blushes a delicate pink. "I don't know…"

I look pointedly behind her. She glances back, her blush deepens. I can't help but roll my eyes before she turns back to me.

"I'll find you," Yuna promises, then grabs the basket of radishes for a hasty exit.

"Being helpful I see," Dylan says from behind me.

"Somewhat. Who is that?" I point to Yuna's retreating figure.

"Yuna? She's like our second in command."

"Well, she's more than that," Rylie chuckles behind his brother.

Dylan scowls.

"You ready to head out?"

"I guess."

Chapter 6

"Gah!"

Scott screams again, smashing an old frame on the floor.

Somehow, someone found our little hole-in-the-wall home and ransacked the place.

Well, I shouldn't say ransacked. The intruders, whoever they may be, only took one thing.

"Where the hell is my sketchpad?" Jacklyn demands, rummaging through every overturned mattress and drawer.

"Who could've done this?" Emmett growls.

"Do you really have to ask?" Rylie barks. "It's gotta be the mongrils!"

"But what would they want with my sketchpad?" Jacklyn whines.

I have a pretty good guess.

"We have to go," I say.

"Wait," Rylie says, grabbing my arm. "What would someone want from that sketchpad?"

"Jacklyn kept sketches of my nightmares."

"So?"

Dylan's eyes meet mine and glaze over. "Me?"

I just nod. "I'm not sure if it's you they are after, though."

"Are you referring to the arm with your name on it?" Scott asked.

"Obviously."

"Hold up. I'm confused." Rylie crosses his arms.

"No time to explain. We need to head back."

I don't wait. They'll follow. Bag on my arm, I jog to the hole in the wall and prepare to shimmy down the makeshift ladder.

And freeze.

My hand flies to my wrist. The scar doesn't tingle.

It *burns*.

"Stop."

Dylan barely halts in time. He shoves into me. I lunge over a horde of wide-eyed infected.

Now, for the two seconds I dangle over this apocalyptic mosh pit, two thoughts cross my mind. 1: How in the hell does a swarm of infected take over the first floor this fast without us recognizing? We'd seen a horde approaching from the north as we entered the building, but there's no way they walked here that fast! This revelation inspired thought number 2: Who knows we are here, and why are they trapping us in with a swarm?

Someone grabs me and I fall back.

"Pull it up!" I scramble to lift the metal frame. Emmett and Dylan clutch an end and yank.

It's heavy. Heavier than expected. Scott and Rylie jump. Pull, yank.

It's up.

And so is an infected.

"Gah!" It thrusts me down and claws at me.

Kick its face. But it's still coming. I can't reach my knife. Kick harder, and flea! But it's got my leg, nails scratching through the jeans and tearing my flesh. Then the bite, scorching the blood faster than it can leave my leg. I scream again.

Someone pulls it off me. It shrieks as it's thrown back down to the first floor.

"Kaiya!" Multiple voices at once. Jacklyn kneels at my leg, ripping the jeans to expose the wound. I growl at her touch.

"Kaiya, you okay?" All five of them are bent over me, but it's Dylan who speaks.

"Just peachy!" I say through gritted teeth.

"Hand me that bottle of water!" Jacklyn orders to someone.

She moves the pantleg back again. I twitch.

"Barely got the muscle," she whispers as I groan.

Barely. *Barely*? Doesn't feel like it barely got me!

"You sure they can't get up here?" Rylie panics.

"They're smart, but not that smart," Scott shoots impatiently. He passes the water bottle to Jacklyn.

Jacklyn flings at the guys to give her room. They all scoot to my head. Except Emmett. He prepares to brace my leg.

"I have to clean it Kaiya," she says. "It's gonna burn."

"Okay."

The moisture turns icy-hot as it hits the cut. I whimper softly, squeezing my eyes. Emmett's stony grasp keeps me from flinching away as the water wicks out the black radiation from the infected person's bite.

Though the burning makes my eyes water, it's not so bad. I've had worse injuries in the past, and I've always healed from them in record time.

"We're gonna have to stay here for the night," Dylan announces. I hadn't noticed he moved until I open my eyes. He's peering down at the infected, alarm evident on his taut jaw, though it does not seep into his voice in the slightest.

Scott grabs my underarms.

"I can move!" I object, but he's already towing me back into the room. The others follow, flipping over the mattresses for seating.

As the sun fades in a sluggish ombre from yellow to orange, then a majestic purple, we listen to the infected snarl below. It's silent for a long time, aside from the occasional 'how do you feel?' and 'are you okay?'

They worry too much.

Before the sunset is replaced by moonlight, my wound feels practically non-existent. Of course, I can't be sure, as Jacklyn has wrapped it tightly in my blue tank. I have strict orders from Scott not to move too much. Worry-wort.

Jacklyn and Emmett snooze on one of the mattresses, snoring softly, when Rylie finally speaks. He sits across the room with his brother, back against the wall, a wary reflection in his eyes.

"Something was mentioned earlier," he says," about your name on an arm?"

I sigh. "It was the day you found us in the woods. We were searching a gas station nearby and found blood and some severed limbs in the women's bathroom. On one of the amputated arms, someone

62

carved my name. It said Kaiya, followed by the number 33."

"What does it mean?" Dylan joins the conversation.

"I don't know. I guess someone knows me. Someone is looking for me."

"You think that's why they took the sketchbook?"

"Maybe. But I'm not worried about whoever it is finding me."

"What were the pictures, exactly?" Rylie asks.

"They were mainly just scenes from my dreams," I start slowly. "I would tell Jacklyn about my nightmares, and she would sketch them out for me, just in case I were to forget. It was never a very clear focus on the person in the dream…until the last entry."

The boys just stare at me. Clearly, they don't understand the gravity of the situation. I readjust myself, squaring my shoulders against the overturned bed frame.

My voice comes quieter now, yet more severe in tone. "Whoever was snooping around up here – the mongrils, Cragen, some other random person who may have carved my name into that arm – I doubt they will be looking for *just* me. They'll be looking for the man who resembles the portrait in that sketchbook. They'll be looking for you, Dylan. And when they find you…"

"What?" he demands harshly. "I can take care of myself; you know."

"How can I know that?" I retort. "I've known you for less than a week. You don't seem to be able to handle yourself in my dreams, so why should I assume it to be any different now?"

"I'm not dead yet. None of it has come true yet."

"Doesn't mean it won't."

We glare at each other darkly. For a brief moment, I imagine I can read his mind. Not so hard when he wears his thoughts on his sleeve the way he does. I know he thinks I've got it all backwards, and it's more a concern about me being able to handle myself. I snicker. If he only knew how well, I could 'take care of myself.' Though, with the minor injury he just witnessed, I can see where he may doubt my capabilities.

Rylie clears his throat. I'm free of Dylan's scrutinizing stare.

"If you two don't mind," Rylie says with a yawn, "I think I'll sleep now. Wake me when it's my watch." Rylie peels himself from the wall and moves to the opposite corner of the room to curl up.

After a few short seconds, he is drooling on his hoodie.

Dylan and I are quiet for a short-lived moment.

"Tell me about your nightmares," I insist.

"I thought you didn't want to hear how you'd die."

"Well, it's obviously not by infected bite, so…" I motion to my leg with a sarcastic smile.

Dylan is silent.

"Or is it by infected?"

He says nothing.

"Do you think it will really happen that way?"

"No," he says too quickly.

I wait, arms crossed.

"It's different each night," he says, his voice tired, but not sleepy. Brown eyes burn with golden torment. "The first one I had of you; I could barely see who you were. You didn't talk or make noise. You were just a blurry woman trying to escape a fire. I felt no connection, no need to help. I just watched.

"The next night was more difficult. A tree was falling towards me. I jumped out of the way. I didn't notice you were there until I turned to inspect the damage. You were pinned under the trunk, wide-eyed, blood pooling around you. I couldn't move to help you. You just stared at me with pleading eyes until you finally laid your head in the dirt."

I gulp. Dylan goes on, ignorant to my discomfort.

"I've watched you drown, burn, fall from cliffs, trip into sharp objects. You've been stabbed, beheaded, had your throat slit, thrown down dark holes, shot with arrows. The dream with the tree was most frequent. But I couldn't save you. It wasn't until the really strange dreams started that your face came clearer to me and I could hear your voice."

I clear the lump in my throat before I ask, "And what were those dreams about?"

Dylan opens his mouth to speak, then snaps his jaw shut.

"I can handle it," I claim.

"Experimentation."

My eyes narrow at him. The weight falls heavier on my chest.

"Why didn't you tell me about this sooner?" I say through gritted teeth. My voice raises an octave as I continue, though I struggle to keep from shouting. "Your theory about Cragen's experiments...*that*'s where you got the theory?"

"It doesn't mean that's what happened."

"And that's how you think I'm going to die?"

He hesitates before uttering "I'm not sure," just low enough for me to hear.

I let out a frustrated *gah* before standing.

"You should rest."

"I'm fine. Doesn't even hurt now." I ignore his concerned gaze and walk out of the room, peering over the hushed horde of confused infected below.

I could do it. Why prolong the inevitable, after all? It would take on step forward, and I could be free of my nightly reminders that he's going to die, I can't stop it, and I'm in the same boat barely floating.

Shut it, Kaiya. I can't afford to think like that. All my energy is to be focused on figuring out what's going on and keeping him alive.

Dylan walks up beside me.

"Whoever took that sketchpad is the reason this horde swarmed the building," I say with a matter-o-fact tone. "And I'm willing to bet they're out there, watching us."

Dylan shrugs. "Maybe not. No one's attacked us yet. Maybe they left after the attempt to flush us out failed. Or maybe it's just a freak incident."

"Maybe. But I don't buy it."

"Don't you think if someone were here to kidnap one of us, they would've done it by now?"

I glare down at the failed trap of snarling creatures. "I suppose."

Dylan's looking down, too, but not at the horde. He's looking at my injured leg. "How long do you think it will take for you to…" he struggles to find the right word. "turn? I assume that's how it works."

I shake my head. "Not for me." I show him the mark on my wrist. "I've had this as long as I can remember. The radiation doesn't affect me, for god-knows what reason." I think about my last words, then amend, "Perhaps it has something to do with your experiment theory."

"Or you're just unique."

"Ha!" I rub my scar subconsciously.

"Does it hurt?"

"Just tingles. Gets like that when I'm near infected."

"Wonder why that is."

I don't answer. I just glare at him sideways.

"I'm not going to let it happen, you know," Dylan says casually. "However, it's supposed to happen. Maybe this will work well for us, knowing all the possibilities."

"Shit?"

"I'll look out for you, and you can attempt to look out for me. That's what I mean."

I laugh. "Whatever you say."

"Do you mind if I...?" he points down at my leg.

I shrug, inching away from the ledge to pull my pantleg back. I rest my foot on his knee so he can undress my wound.

He gasps. "How?"

"I heal fast," is all I say.

"Guess you don't need this anymore," he says, throwing the blue shirt to the infected.

The thin shirt drifts down to the dead the way my hope drifts out of my chest. The same shirt I wore on the day I woke up two and a half years ago, and it's gone. Maybe it's some twisted symbol for who I was then. That confused, frightened girl is long gone, too. Devoured by this new world.

"Guess not."

****

The drive back to the community is a long and stressful one. Rylie suggested we travel on foot through the woods so it would be harder for anyone spying on us to follow, but I was obligated to point out how easily someone could pick us off, one by one, if we hoof it. This seemed to change his mind. Different story with his brother's neck on the line, along with his own.

"It's been a while since we've trained," Scott complains in a casual tone, resting an arm along the seat headrest behind me. Instinctively, I lean forward. He doesn't seem to notice.

"I kinda miss it."

"Trained?" Dylan asks.

"Work out," Emmett clarifies. "Practice the art of killing, defensive tactics, kick some ass, that sort of thing?"

"I know what train means," Dylan snaps. Then, more civil, "But didn't you guys do that just two days ago? How often do you train?"

"Usually every morning, unless we're too tired."

"You know, we have a gym in the community building. You guys are welcome to use it."

"Man, if only we were allowed *inside* the building," I say, glowering at Rylie. His smirk in the rearview mirror grows wider.

"I only said the people wouldn't want you staying in there, not that you weren't allowed in," Rylie says from the driver's seat. The van slows to a crawl.

"Seriously, though, let me know when you guys want to train. I could use a good sparring partner."

Emmett and Scott exchange strange look, then burst into laughing fits. I struggle not to snicker myself, because I know they are imagining what it would be like to beat his arrogant rear to the ground. Surprisingly, Rylie isn't set off by our laughter. His mouth remains glued in the same curly grin as we enter the community gates.

"Dylan!" Yuna skips to the van as we pull up. She embraces him long and hard. "You guys were supposed to come back yesterday. What happened?"

"Complications," is all he says, pulling away awkwardly.

"Well, thank god you're all back. We have a situation."

"What's going on?" I ask, but it is as if I haven't spoken.

"Kedrick left."

Kedrick? Who's Kedrick?

"Ran off? What do you mean?"

"He got worried when you didn't return," Yuna explains. "He left at nightfall to look for you, even though I insisted he wait until morning. He's still not back." Her pupils shine deep with concern, deeper than a bottomless pit.

"That's her brother," Dylan whispers as an aside to me.

"He said he was going to get some supplies on his run. I figured he'd be back by now."

Dylan puts a comforting hand on her shoulder. "I'm sure he's fine. Maybe he's trying to find a car or something to bring back the goods. Worst case scenario, he's hauled up somewhere like we were and will be back when it's safe."

Rylie creases his brows at his brother. Their eyes are locked before Rylie nods. "Yes," he says, still looking at Dylan. "I'm sure he'll be back tomorrow morning. If he's not back by first light, we'll go get him."

"Why don't we look for him now?" I ask.

"Because he's fine. I'm sure of it," Dylan says. "He has a long-distance radio. He'd call for help if he needed it. Besides, you're still healing."

"What? No, I'm no-"

Dylan stomps on my toes. I glare at him.

Yuna looks from him to me, then back again.

"We'll get him at first light if he's not back," Dylan confirms.

Yuna sighs, then retreats back to the building.

Once she's out of range, I punch Dylan in the arm.

"I'm really fine."

Dylan positions himself in front of me and leans in so close I can feel the heat from his skin. His coffee eyes smolder me. I'm stuck.

"I just need an excuse," he breathes. "There really is nothing to worry about. Her brother leaves a lot, usually for days at a time, just so he can get away from Yuna."

"But what about the mongrils, or whoever tried to trap us?"

"He can handle himself. We need to strategize before we just wonder off into the occupied woods again."

"So tomorrow, then?"

Dylan sighs and tilts away. "I should go check on her."

And he walks away.

My feet refuse to move. Not because his proximity shocked me – though it did, in ways that I've never experienced before – but because I have trouble processing his strange behavior. Granted, I don't know Dylan well, but his responses don't seem normal.

Though my previous injury is nothing but a tiny scar now, I can still feel my blood attempting to boil out the leftover toxicity from the bite. My eyes droop, my forehead inflamed, and my body overwhelmed with fatigue, as it typically does after an infected bite – yes, I've been snapped at more times than I care to remember…at times, it has been inevitable for me when getting us out of sticky situations.

To avoid being chastised, especially by Scott, I hastily excuse myself to the tent for a power nap.

And man, do I regret it.

Chapter 7

My nightmares the last few nights have been manageable. Maybe it's this place, or Dylan's presence, that's suppressed the prophetic incidents.

Until now.

I'm walking through the woods, shouting his name at the top of my lungs. Worry burns my throat more each time I say it.

I reach the top of a hill. His grunts grow closer. He's at the base, fighting off a couple infected in the afternoon sunlight.

Surely, he wouldn't go down like this.

And I'm right. By the time I get to the hill's base, he's already killed them both with little-to-no struggle.

Dylan turns to smile at me, a triumphant smile only broken by small pants that escape his lips. His eyes are bright with excitement. Or adrenaline. Whichever. The irises are a caramel color now, more golden, and wilder than I've seen them. When the sunlight hits just right, they seem to catch fire, burning a brilliant, spiced pigment.

This is my new favorite color.

I'm mesmerized. By his eyes. His smile. Him. And he's observing me, too.

A sickening crack breaks the air between us. We look up at the same time.

I'm not sure how. I don't know what caused it.

A tree falls toward us.

Dylan shoves me backward, just as he has before, the same strange current buzzing through my shoulders and down my frame as I plummet.

Deafening thud, followed by his painful cry.

I can't peel myself from the ground to pull him out or lift the tree. I can do nothing. Nothing but watch the color in his eyes fade to a dull brown, fading still as they close permanently.

****

The tent spins. My sleeping bag clings to me like a sweaty t-shirt. I peel it off gingerly and sit up only to place my head between my knees. The spinning slows, as does my breathing.

The glow from outside the tent reveals the setting sun. *How long have I been sleeping?* Scott and Jacklyn chatter outside the tent, a faint crackling of a fire filling brief moments of silence. I wait for the nightmare to completely subside before I join them.

But I don't get the chance to exit my tent. The door unzips, and Yuna steps in.

"Hi, sleepy," she greets me, her voice still sweet as honey.

"Hey." My own voice sounds groggy as hell.

"I don't have much time," she says, crouching down in front of me.

"You have information, I take it?"

73

"Sort of. I have some old stories for you later, but I figured you'd want to hear the latest scoop first."

"Let's hear it."

"Dylan's leaving tomorrow." Yuna's mouth forms a tight line. "He's asked a few of us to stay behind and babysit you."

"What? Babysit me?"

"He's going to look for my brother, I think, and get supplies. He doesn't want you to leave, I guess because of something that happened while you were out?"

I curse silently.

"Everyone knows he's going, but no one is supposed to tell you." Her whispers are rushed. "So don't say anything."

"But it's not safe for him to go, not now," I complain.

"Why? What's going on?" Her brows furrow. The crease in her forehead sinks deeper.

"I can't say. Don't worry. I'll take care of it. Nothing will happen."

Yuna gives me a scrutinizing look, one I hope I won't have to see again.

She finally nods. "Alright." Footsteps approaching the fire cuts our conversation short. "I'll have more information for you later!" Then she rushes from the tent.

I twiddle my thumbs for a moment as I collect my thoughts. Dylan isn't making my job easy. How am I supposed to keep him safe if he puts himself in harm's way and leaves me behind? How do I prevent my dream from coming true from here?

Guess it's a good thing I'm stealthy, I think before I join the others around the fire.

I'll just have to sneak out and follow him.

"She's finally up!" Scott laughs and points at my crazy hair. I chuck a stick at him. Of course, he dodges it with as much grace as a dancer. I throw my wavy knots into a sloppy bun and sit beside him. Dylan sits on my other side and offers me a tinfoil food packet. I call them hobo dinners.

His proximity makes it hard to concentrate on my own thoughts. I know my irritation towards him is palpable, and I can feel him staring at me questioningly, but pay him no heed.

Scott repeatedly slaps at the awkward cluster of hair on my head as I eat. The third time, I can feel his arm extending behind me. I turn to snatch his wrist and twist. He cries out, as do Jacklyn and Emmett. Scott sounds like a wounded schoolgirl while Jacklyn and Emmett's wails resemble that of hyenas.

"Don't poke the bear!" Jacklyn cackles.

But Dylan is not laughing. His eyes lock on the back of my neck.

My hand flies back to cover it. I've almost forgotten about my mark. I wonder for a brief moment how much of the twisting black vines shows. It must be visible. Dylan continues to stare. I shy closer to Scott and hoist my shirt to rest higher on my shoulder blades.

"Are you okay?" Jacklyn eyes me warily. She's the only other person who knows about my mark, and I intend to keep it that way.

I nod. "Just chilly."

"I can get more fuel for the fire," Scott offers.

"I'll go with you."

We leave to the line of trees casting darkness on the outer wall. Scott grabs some fallen branches, his triumphant smile evident. Why is he so smug?

"Can I ask a huge favor?" I say in the sweetest voice I can conjure.

"Anything," he vows. Always so willing.

"Can you and Jacklyn trade tents tonight?"

That stuns him. His smile slips. "Why?" His brows knit together. "Do I make you uncomfortable or something?"

"No. Jacklyn's just more comforting when it comes to my nightmares."

"Oh. Sure."

Man, I must be getting good at this lying thing.

As the night goes on, I can't shake the feeling of Dylan's eyes on my neck. Self-conscious? Maybe. But I do catch him looking at me from time to time. He fails at being discrete. His slow reflexes do him no favors in this area, either.

One by one, the others exit the campfire circle to sleep. Dylan, Scott, Jacklyn, and I are the last up. The fire burns low now.

Scott reluctantly gives in to sleep. He puts a hand on my arm and leans close. Dylan and Jacklyn watch us curiously.

"I'm going to hit the hay," Scott says. His hand slides down my arm as he stands. "Goodnight."

I shiver once he turns away.

"Hey, why is he going to Emmett's tent?" Jacklyn demands.

"I asked him to."

Her mouth opens to form a question, but my stare silences her.

"You and Scott share a tent?" Dylan asks. A hint of resentment seeps into his voice.

"We didn't really have an option. You only gave us the two tents."

"Right. Sorry."

Jacklyn clears her throat. She and Dylan stare at each other for a moment. As if he can read her mind, he suddenly stands to stretch.

"I better go to sleep, too. Goodnight Jacklyn...Kaiya." His eyes bore through mine for two seconds, then he disappears into the dark.

"We're alone, right?" Jacklyn asks quietly.

I strain my ears, but only hear the crackling from the fire and distant groans hundreds of yards away.

I nod to her. "Can you check it?"

Of course, she knows what I mean. She jumps to her feet and walks behind me, brushing my hair away from my neck.

"How bad is it?"

"It's darker now." Her voice is blank. "About an inch from your hair."

I sigh.

"We have to find something to stop it from growing."

"I know," I say. "And I think I know where we might find some answers."

"Really?"

"Something Dylan and Rylie said that first day here got me thinking. I don't know for certain, of course, but *he* might know something about what's going on with me."

"Who? Where do we need to go?"

"Cragen's compound."

77

Chapter 8

The fire is gone, but the ashes still glow a brilliant red. The air grows chilly and crisp. Only my thoughts keep me company now. Thoughts about protecting Dylan from the afternoon treefall ahead, of the growing sting in my neck, and of what I might find at Cragen's compound. How will I convince Dylan to show us the way? How will I sneak in? How will I keep Dylan safe from whatever might lie there?

I smother the embers in dirt and head towards my tent.

I notice a candle still lit in Dylan and Rylie's camper, which stops me. Weren't they going to sleep? I don't have to strain to hear them arguing from within.

Curiosity wins. I tiptoe to the camper and make myself a statue under their cracked window.

"Do you really think she is in danger?" It's Rylie's voice.

"I know she is," Dylan whispers. "That's why we can't let her go tomorrow."

"But I don't understand. Why do you want to protect someone you don't know? And how do you know she is in danger?"

I can hear Dylan's heart thump unsteadily inside the camper.

"I had another nightmare last night."

"About her dying again?"

"She was walking alone in the woods, and Cragen and the mongrils show up. They stab her, then take her away."

The two are silent for a moment. The dread is heavy, even out here.

"In the dream, was she close to the community?"

"I don't think so," Dylan says slowly. "But it's hard to tell. The whole thing was stranger than normal."

"What do you mean?"

Dylan's words are spoken with utmost caution. "Most of the time, I'm forced to watch her die, and I know she's dead before I wake up. I can sometimes hear her last breath. But this time, Cragen drags her away before she is unconscious, and she's yelling for us to run."

"That's a good thing, isn't it?" Rylie's tone grows hopeful. "She doesn't die in the dream. Maybe she won't die if Cragen gets ahold of her."

"Or is it worse?" Dylan tests. "God only knows what he would do to her in the safety of his compound."

Rylie doesn't answer, but there is palpable skepticism clouding his calm.

"Do you really think it would be any worse than what the mongrils did to you?"

Is Rylie referring to the experimentations the mongrils did on his brother, or something else? I wonder if experimentation and torture go hand in hand inside Cragen's compound.

"Why would I dream about it if it weren't of dire importance? Just listen to me. She is not leaving the walls."

"I'm pretty sure she can take care of herself, Dylan."

Dylan groans. "Will you just keep an eye on her tomorrow? Please?"

"Fine, jeez!"

"Thank you."

Rylie mumbles something unintelligible. Then, louder, "I don't understand why you don't just tell her, man. She's heard about the other nightmares."

"No one wants to hear that they are going to die," Dylan says glumly. And, of course, he knows this to be true more than anyone. "She's heard it before, I know. But this time is different. I can feel it. Plus, if I tell her, she'll probably weasel her way outside like the crazy person she is. I won't have her blood on *my* hands."

And I don't need to hear anymore.

Dylan must be crazy, thinking he cann*ot* include me in tomorrow's venture. My capture can be avoided. In this moment, I'm sure of that much. I've been stealthy around the mongrils before. I can avoid them. His fate in the afternoon sunlight, though, is a different story.

But is it wrong that I think the situation is funny?

Not the possibility of me dying, or of Dylan dying. It's the idea of Dylan trying to prevent my death. I doubt Dylan will be able to do anything about it! If I am to die, then he won't be able to save me.

I have strange senses – like the twinge in my scar around infected – and fast reflexes. What does Dylan have? An attitude? A good heart? Prophetic dreams? *Ha!* Yeah, that should be enough to protect the both of us! Don't get me wrong, it's sweet that he doesn't want me to die…but honestly, what is the boy going to do to stop it?

At least it is different for him. I'm more than confident in my ability to keep him safe, even though the images of his crumpled body still blur my sight occasionally.

He will not die.

No one wants to hear that they are going to die.

Ain't that the truth, I think back to myself.

And then it finally clicks in my brain. Why it hadn't clicked before, I'm not sure, but it certainly does now. Perhaps it is because my lifeline is drawing to its end, destiny and doom weighing down on me now like a falling brick building waiting to crash into the unsuspecting cement.

I'm going to *die*. And soon.

****

I only get an hour of sleep that night.

In that hour, I have yet another nightmare.

The room is dim, stuffy, and quiet, aside from the occasional staticky flicker of the dome light above me. I can't move. I can't speak. I can barely even breathe. I roll my eyes to look down the slanted table at my body. I'm strapped at the ankles, wrists, and waist. As I inhale, I can feel one loosely resisting strap running over my neck. Strange wires and tubes extend from my arms. The purple and blue veins stick out harshly against my ghost-white skin. I look like a corpse!

But I'm not alone.

There are two other people strapped to gurneys on either side of me. I don't realize until I hear them moving. They must be trying to wiggle free from the wrist and ankle guards.

With as much strength as I can muster, I'm able to move my head.

I turn to the right…

It's Dylan.

And to the left…

Rylie.

I try to ask them if they're okay, but my voice is missing yet again. I have an IV on my right arm, and a long bandage covering my left arm. I'm almost completely numb. Neither Dylan nor Rylie have IV's…why do I have one?

"Kaiya? Are you okay?" Dylan asks. He seems relatively calm.

Again, I open my mouth to speak. No words.

The sound of a door swinging shut makes Rylie flinch. He struggles harder against the restraints. Two people enter the room. One of them is a doctor, and the other is –

"Scott! Hey man!" Rylie exclaims. "Get us out of here!"

But Scott ignores him. He stops in front of my gurney and looks down at me with a weird, distorted grin plastered to his now pale face. Then, he turns to Dylan.

The blonde doctor wheels a metal table between Dylan and I, then sits a tool tray on top. Scott picks up a permanent red marker from the tray and lifts Dylan's shirt. He draws an X over Dylan's navel.

Scott then reaches for the scalpel.

"No!" Rylie bellows. He thrashes on the gurney like an angry fish out of water. The doctor stomps to him and tightens the manacles.

But somehow Rylie gets a hand free. He reaches up to rip the mask off the doctor's face, revealing a white scar that runs from the doctor's cheekbone to his chin. I recognize him immediately not only by the blemish, but by the picture I carry with me.

It's Cragen.

Before we can react, Dylan howls out in pain. His scream pierces my eardrums. Rylie screams alongside him. I want to scream, too.

****

"Jesus, woman, wake up!"

I gasp, eyes fly open, and sit up. My head smacks something hard.

"Ow," I complain, rubbing my brow. "What the hell?"

"Sorry, sorry," Dylan apologizes, also massaging his bruised head.

"What the *hell* are you doing in here? What happened?"

"You were screaming, then you head-butted me."

"I was?"

"Yeah, pretty loud too," he says, sitting down in front of the zipped-up door. "I'm surprised you didn't wake up anyone else. Man, you've got a set of lungs! Must have been some nightmare."

I think of Dylan on the gurney, Cragen towering over him and his brother as the screams ensued.

"Yeah," I admit. "It was. Where's Jacklyn?"

"She's helping inside."

It's quiet for a long time. We look at each other for several minutes. Dylan looks deep in thought as he watches me. It should make me uncomfortable. But I'm watching him too. His light eyes are tired and tormented. I listen to his unsteady heartbeat as I learn his face. I hadn't noticed the faded freckles before. They complement his hair well.

"Do you think you can trust someone without knowing them long?" he asks.

"I'm not sure," I answer. "I've trained myself over the years not to trust outsiders, especially after meeting the mongrils. But I'll get back to you on that."

He lets his eyes wander as he thinks.

"Are you like this with everyone?" I blurt. I'm not sure why I ask when I already know the answer.

He chuckles. "Like what?"

"So nosy and…chivalrous, I guess? No, that's not the right word. Hmm…"

"What do you mean?"

I try my best to explain myself without giving away the fact that I overheard him yesterday. "You're acting protective over me, and I don't like it."

"Oh." He doesn't bother denying it. "Why not?"

"Because I'm not used to it. And I don't need protecting. I know how to take care of myself. It just doesn't make sense because we don't know each other.

Which makes me think that you're like this with everyone."

He shakes his head. "You're wrong."

"About which part?"

"All of it," he says. He repositions himself so he sits cross-legged in front of me, closer than I expect him to be. "I have no doubt you can take care of yourself, but you do need protected. And I can't explain it, but I feel like I *do* know you. Maybe not as well as I should, but I know who you are."

"You think you've got me all figured out, don't you?" I mock him.

He leans forward. Our faces are inches apart.

"Maybe I do," he grins.

"After such a short time? I doubt it."

"You'd be surprised. And no, I'm not like that with everyone."

"Wow, I should feel *so* special."

To that he does not reply. I lean away from him.

"I get it, though," I say.

"Get what?"

"I feel like I know you, too. And Rylie."

He smiles. "Don't tell your boyfriend that. He might get the wrong idea."

"You mean Scott?"

"Yeah. He looks like a teddy bear on steroids."

"He's my best friend."

"Ah," he breathes. "Friend-zoned. Poor guy."

"Can't help it," I shrug. "You can't force feelings for someone."

"You're right," Dylan agrees. "Those come naturally, or they don't come at all."

Again, awkward silence.

I try to break the tension by pointing out the obvious. "This…" I motion at the two of us with my index finger, "this is weird. Really weird."

"Why? Because you don't know me?"

I shake my head. My hair bounces in front of my face. "I'm not sure if it's that or the fact that I've had nightmares about you dying for a few years, but it's definitely weird."

"A good weird or bad weird?" Dylan asks.

Good question. "A strange weird."

Just then, Jacklyn unzips the tent and steps in. She looks at the two of us, confused, then begins to blush on my behalf.

"Sorry, am I interrupting something?" she giggles.

"Nope," I answer too quick, unnecessary emphasis on the *P*. I look pointedly at Dylan. He nods in understanding.

"I'll go wake up Rylie," Dylan excuses himself.

Jacklyn plops down gracefully beside me. She's such a happy person in the mornings. Makes me sick.

"What was that about?" she asks with a wink.

"Nothing, he heard me screaming in my sleep."

"Oh."

I shrug my jacket and shoes on in a rush. Jacklyn watches me suspiciously.

"Where are you going?"

"To make sure he doesn't do anything stupid."

"Like what?"

Like running out to find a dead man, all just to be pulverized by a tree.

Jacklyn speaks again.

"Can't you just let him make his own mistakes?"

How can I, knowing full well what may happen if I leave him alone? There's no blood on these hands, and I plan to keep it that way.

"I figured as much," Jacklyn whispers in response to my silence.

I wiggle my way around her and out of the tent.

But the camper is empty. Dylan and Rylie are gone.

"Damnit!" I slam the camper door behind me.

At this exact moment, sirens wail from the building.

"They have fucking sirens?" Jacklyn covers her ears.

"What's going on?"

The sirens continue to wail. I climb atop the camper for a better view.

A crowd forms in front of the western gate with more residents running towards the commotion. I spot Yuna below, jogging from the fields to the crowd.

"Yuna!" I shout. She stops to look at me. "What is it?"

"Someone's outside the gate!"

I jump down to rejoin Jacklyn. We follow Yuna to the community entrance.

The gate creaks open.

Mongrils.

Fifty or sixty armed mongrils.

And they're not alone.

Black-haired Blair smiles when she spots me pushing through the crowd. Dylan kneels in front of her, her hands on his shoulders, his mouth taped shut and eyes wide with panic. Rylie lies on the ground beside him. Must be knocked out. I can see him breathe.

But no one is looking at them. Everyone's focused on the tree line three yards out, where a noose swing.

With a blonde-haired teenager tied at the end.

"Kedrick?!" Yuna rushes forward. The people closest restrain her. She crumbles in the dirt, sobbing uncontrollably.

"Blair," I growl.

"You remembered my name," she says in her booming tone. "How sweet."

"You bitch!" Yuna screams. "You'll pay!" I can't understand her words after that. Her threats drift back into broken cries.

"Relax. This isn't a social visit," Blair assures her. "We're looking for someone."

"So, you never found your special someone," Jacklyn snarls. "Have you tried looking in hell?"

Blair ignores her snark.

"Cragen is looking for patient 33, otherwise known as Kaiya."

And then it clicks. Not from her speaking, but from the tattered, blood-splattered blue shirt dangling from Blair's fingers. How did she get it? Dylan tossed it to the infected.

Oh boy.

So, Dylan's theory may not be far off base.

Dylan stares at me, eyes pleading me to keep quiet. A lump form hard and dry in my throat.

"We've tracked her this far, so we know she's here," Blair says when no one speaks. "Hand her over and we will spare these two."

Okay, so Dylan's theory may be directly on base, minus some mystery details. Otherwise, how could she have tracked me, and why does she have that shirt?

Dylan shakes his head.

I sigh.

"Promise you'll leave everyone alone, and I'll come quietly."

Blair releases her hold on Dylan and crosses her arms with a sharp laugh. "You? *You* are patient 33?"

I shrug. "I guess so." But I'm not looking at her as I talk.

"We've been searching a long time for you."

"Well, you have me now," I step forward. "So let them go."

Blair cuts Dylan's arms free and rips the tape from his mouth, then shoves him toward me. He grabs my arms to steady himself, lingering too close for a moment longer.

"What are you doing?" he hisses. "We can take them."

I shake my head. "You know that's not how it's destined to go down." Dylan glares at me. "Don't you dare follow us."

"But you'll…"

I slap a hand over his mouth.

"Let. It. Go."

I walk around him, past Rylie passed out in the threshold, and offer Blair my hands. She binds them in zip ties.

"Kaiya!" Scott's pushing past people. Jacklyn stops him.

Blair orders the mongrils onward, I assume in the direction of Cragen's compound. I chance a look back to the gates.

The community people have dispersed, retreating to their duties. Five people remain at the entrance, staring at me with desperate eyes. Except Yuna. She's still holding herself in the fetal position, looking past us at her brother's dangling corpse.

"Move." Blair pushes me in the direction of her men. I tear my eyes away from my friends.

I'm sorry, I think to them.

And I am.

Sorry it came to this. That Rylie and Dylan were captured over me. That Kedrick had to pay with his life. That my family for the last two or so years has to watch me being escorted away. That I have to see their faces twisted this way as I am forced to leave them.

I don't know what Cragen wants me for or why any of this had to happen, but I know one thing for certain.

My life isn't worth any of this.

And after I get my answers, Cragen and the mongrils will pay.

Chapter 9

"If you're thinking of escaping, you can forget it," says Blair.

We've been walking for most of the day. We stop for an hour at a creek where her men drink and bathe in the water. The mongrils play in the creek much like children, galivanting through its light current and laughing like psychos let out of a looney bin. Traveling with a group as manic as them makes me nervous. Not for myself, but for any others they come across.

"If I wanted to escape, I would have already."

"So confident," she barks a laugh.

"What does Cragen want with me?"

Blair rolls her eyes and leans back on her elbows. We sit by the bank, watching the mongrils act like...well, mongrils.

"He won't say. The only thing I know is that you are valuable to him."

"Valuable?"

Blair nods. "I can't say anything else. I'm sure Cragen will catch you up to speed, after he gets what he wants."

"And what does he want?"

"You'll find out soon enough."

I groan.

****

After another few hours of trudging along, the sun begins to set. My scar stings savagely. Infected roam our circumference with only a one-hundred-yard radius from us. My hands are bound. I have no weapons. Yes, I am surrounded by armed mongrils, but that fact only makes me more anxious.

Then the rain starts.

Blair giggles at me. "You're not worm-food yet. We have a safe place up ahead."

We escape the rain in a crumbling factory building. The mongrils split up to barricade the doors and windows while Blair and one of her henchmen escort me up the north wall staircase. We stop on the second-floor landing. Blair hands the man something and gives him instructions to tie me up. Only a few feet from my containment is a door. I have no clue where it leads, but the mongrils don't bother boarding it up. Must be to a long-gone balcony. If that's the case, there is no way in or out using that door, unless I want to fall two stories into god-knows-what.

I'll take my chances.

The henchman, a bulky bald guy, cuts the first zip tie from my wrists to retie me. Rookie mistake. I kick him hard in the shin and shove him to the wall. Diving to the door, I open it.

I was right. There used to be a balcony. Now there's sharp shards of metal jutting from the brick wall. Not to mention, a horde of eager infected below.

I catch myself in the doorframe. Two arms pull me back, twist me till I'm back inside, pinned to the wall.

I spit in his face.

He punches me.

I fall, hand to my throbbing cheek, head spinning.

The man shoves me harshly to a seated position, then proceeds to double strap me to the rail with another zip tie and a pair of policeman handcuffs. Before retreating, he slams the door shut and mutters *bitch* under his breath.

"Take the second squad with you," I overhear Blair order him as they stomp down the stairs. "Tell Cragen we have her. Then circle around for her friends, should we miss any."

"I'm sorry?"

"Orders are orders," she says softly. "He needs more than one guinea pig."

"And what will you do?"

Blair lowers her voice, but I can still make it out. "Kaiya's friends have been tracking us. They will come for her soon. I will apprehend as many as possible, assuming the first squad doesn't kill them all first. I think Cragen will be pleased to see some familiar faces amongst the test subjects."

They're coming for me?

"As you wish." The man took thirty or so mongrils with him, venturing into the downpour.

Shit.

I specifically told Dylan *not* to follow. What is he thinking?

And what did Blair mean by guinea pigs and test subjects? Exactly what kind of experiments is Cragen planning to perform?

93

The night is long and harsh. Blair sends three men every hour or so to do a perimeter check. Most of the time, only two come back. I imagine the ones that don't return must be dead. Killed by infected, most likely. Or, perhaps, they are forming an ambush for Dylan and the others.

The mongrils grow tired quickly. They take shifts, one or two of them up for watch at a time. Blair sleeps the entire night.

During the last shift, though, the only mongril taking watch falls asleep at the bottom step. I'm not sure he's out until his snores vibrate the railing. The sun has just barely risen, soft blonde rays peeking through the boarded windows.

Perfect opportunity.

The zip ties are easy enough to break, but the cuffs are too tight. I can't wiggle my hands free enough to break the ties. I don't have hairpins to pick the lock. The railing is weak enough I could kick it away to relieve the cuffs, but the ruckus would certainly wake every sleeping mongril in the factory.

So, there is no escape plan.

The door on the second level creaks, but not loud enough to wake anyone. I adjust myself quickly, preparing to connect my left boot with whatever may come through.

But then I hear my name.

"Need a hand?"

"Dylan! How did you…what are you doing?!" I scold him quietly.

"Getting you out of here." He scrambles through the door. I'm surprised at how quiet he is as he sneaks to my side.

Dylan places his hands on my shoulders and looks at me, scanning for injuries. He takes in my bruised cheek. I turn away. I expect him to shrug it off and cut me free, but he doesn't right away.

He hugs me first.

Yeah, because *now* is the time to hug.

"Why did you come?" I demand.

"I thought we agreed to help protect each other?" He pulls back and scrambles for something in his pocket.

I scowl. "I told you not to follow. Blair knew you were coming. It's a trap."

"Then we better get you out fast," he says, working a pick into the cuffs.

After three seconds of jiggling, the cuffs click free. Dylan whips out his pocketknife to relieve the zip tie. I jump to my feet.

"How'd you get in?"

Dylan grins. The door swings open.

A staircase of infected corpses greets us. Dylan steps at a slant to avoid the sharp metal, then offers me a hand.

"HEY!"

Shit.

"Time to go!" Dylan yanks me by the arm. I fly over the collapsed balcony and roll down the corpse mound. My head smacks the ground violently.

"Kaiya!" A new voice. Several rushing footsteps.

"Scott?"

They're all here. Dylan. Scott. Jacklyn. Emmett. I'm shocked to see Rylie amongst them, but of course he wouldn't let his brother come alone.

Multiple hands pull me up. Mongrils shout inside.

"Come on!" they start back towards the creek.

"Wrong way," I shout.

"What? No, it's not," Rylie barks.

"Cragen's compound is this way!" I point around the factory at the second squad's tracks.

"You want to go *towards* him?!"

"I have to," I retort. "I need answers."

Five pairs of eyes glare at me. I can hear the mongrils scrambling about.

"We don't have time for this," I snap. "I'm going *this* way. Feel free to join me."

I know they will follow before they do. Dylan runs ahead in an attempt to lead.

But as we rear the far corner, Dylan is struck with the buttstock of a rifle. He falls.

Blair saunters out, rifle awkward in her arms. She spins the rifle like a baton until the barrel stares Dylan in the face.

I slam into her full force before she can pull the trigger.

We tumble. The rifle is lost.

She straddles me, knuckles fly to my face. I block with my arms and pull her down to me, rolling until *I* straddle *her*. My fist power-drives her face once, twice, but the third is deflected. Swing, miss. Blair wedges her knees to my chest and shoves. I stagger up.

Blair stands, dramatically spitting blood at her feet. The other mongrils – all seven of them – come charging out of the building, weapons poised. My group stands two feet from me. Scott glances at the rifle, but I hold a hand to him and the others. No need to get themselves killed on my account.

"Stand back, she's mine!" Blair barks, wiping her lip.

She stares at me for a second, eyes wild. "Cragen wants you alive," she growls and digs into her back pocket. "But I can always just say the infected got you first."

She flips out a switch blade and dives at me. I dodge to the right. She cuts through the air, slicing hard to the side. Misses me, but just barely. I hear the fabric on the back of my shirt tear at the same second that I feel the breeze of the knife. She swipes again. I dip sideways, grab her arm, and twist. The knife clashes to the dirt.

I reach for it, but she grabs my collar, ripping my shirt farther up. With a loud *huff*, she pulls me backwards.

I crash into a trunk, sending several loud pops up my spine. I try to lunge forward, but the sting in my back sends me to the ground. I don't turn my neck in fear of damaging my spine further, but I hear several feet pounding the earth towards me. Somewhere in the distance – *But is it in the distance? I can't tell. So dizzy...* – I can make out the impatient snarls of approaching infected.

I try to stand again, but the shooting pain sends me down. I roll over to a crawling position and try to inch away into the tree line, but I'm met with a cold boot to my backbone.

"I don't believe this," Blair says with a hesitant laugh.

What is she going on about? Then I realize. My mark is exposed.

Blair kneels beside me, taking a fistful of my hair. She yanks me to her level.

"You're not worth killing now, anyway," she sneers in my ear, then squeals and jumps away.

I collapse, turning onto my aching backside to see Dylan with the knife, the edge lightly coated in Blair's blood. Dylan hands the knife to Rylie, who disappears from my line of sight as Scott and Emmett pull me to my feet. I howl.

Now that I'm up, I take a second to absorb the massacre happening behind the scenes. The few mongrils left in Blair's first squad have been overrun by infected. The creatures don't even seem to notice us only ten yards away, though a couple have broken off from the binging group to check out the commotion, only to be met with Jacklyn's superior monster-killing skills. And boy, does she look like a bad-ass whipping that red hair around while she slice-n-dices the mass. So sweet and petite, yet so deadly.

Emmett and Scott turn me gently to face Blair, braced against a tree, cupping the gash down the length of her previously injured cheek. Despite the burn she must feel as the blood trickles to her chin, she laughs.

"I'm going to the compound," I say. She stops laughing. "And Cragen's not going to know I'm coming."

"We'll see about that," she spits.

"Why did you hesitate?" Emmett demands, jabbing a finger at Blair. "You said you were going to...so why didn't you kill her?"

Blair cackles manically, pointing at me. "Just look at you!" she laughs louder, then stops abruptly, eyes burning. "You don't have long, anyway."

Jacklyn runs past us, punches Blair, and then tugs on Emmett's arm.

"We have to go. Now."

****

We travel at a relatively fast pace considering my injuries. Dylan and Scott each have an arm around me for support. It's not until we've put several miles between the factory and us that we decide to stop.

"Just give me a second," I reassure the group. "It's not broken, I don't think. Just strained and a little out of place." Like I said before, I heal quickly.

They're all silent. Their glares burn holes in my face.

"What?" I finally ask.

Scott clears his throat. "Kaiya, what's that black thing on your back?"

My teeth gnash. "You saw it?"

They all nod.

"I don't know what it is, to be totally honest."

"Blair seemed to know something about it," Rylie points out.

I shrug, then groan. Not a pain-free motion. "Whatever it is, it's not good."

They still stare, waiting for some sort of explanation.

With a sigh, I turn to peel my torn shirt back, revealing my darkening spine.

"It started small," I say in a small voice I don't recognize, "like an inch-long grey mark down here." I trace the area on my lower back, which sends I strange wave of warmth up the mark. "It grows a little every month and sends a burning sensation through me every time."

"When did you first notice it?" Scott asks.

"Over two and a half years ago," I admit, though it sounds like a question. Scott's facial muscles tighten. "I felt the pain, and Jacklyn checked it out for me. As it worms up my back, the burning becomes more pronounced."

"Why didn't you tell me?" Scott demands before I finish. "You told Jacklyn, but you didn't tell me?!" He shoots an accusatory finger at Emmett. "Did he know?"

Emmett holds his arms up. "It's all new info to me, man."

"And what about *him*?" Scott juts his chin at Dylan. "Did you tell him?"

"I haven't told anyone but Jacklyn because I don't know what it is," I say. "It could be nothing."

We all grow silent for a moment. Scott's aura softens, but not drastically. Some strain in my back eases, too.

"You good?" Dylan asks. His voice sounds rough against the hostile silence.

"It's getting better," I say with a huff.

Dylan steps toward me, stripping his t-shirt. This moment reminds me of a cheesy situation I used to read about in romance novels, where the lure from a man becomes overwhelming after his chest is bare. One of many, many reasons I've hated romance as long as I can remember. The clichés are nearly unbearable. Luckily, Dylan sports a tank underneath. His undergarment is the only thing to stifle my adolescent giggle.

"Here," he says, holding it out to me.

"Thanks," I say with an awkward clearing of my throat. My fingers graze his hand, the brief touch a staticky heat. I recoil slightly, but he doesn't seem to notice. Before I can even ask, everyone turns to face the opposite direction so I can peel off my ruined garment and replace it with Dylan's green tee. The shirt is noticeably warm and smells of his natural, dirty musk. I try to ignore it as each movement wafts in my face.

After our short rest ends, we continue to follow the tracks left from the second squad of mongrils. I had hoped we'd walk through the forest in relative silence so I can gather my thoughts and create a game plan for slipping into the compound. That is not the case. It feels like I have a line of bodyguards. Scott walks a few paces ahead of me – he claims it's because he's the best tracker, but I know he's suspicious of Dylan and Rylie...or is it some strange form of jealousy that applies to strained friendship? – and Dylan and Rylie follow closely at my flanks. Jacklyn and Emmett file lazily behind us. Once in a while, I hear Emmett complain about Jacklyn not walking fast enough. Guess he doesn't like 'bringing up the rear where he can't hear the juicy stuff.' That comment makes me snicker. He also wonders aloud to a different person every few minutes about what is going on with our little formation in front of the herd. Of course, Jacklyn tells him to shut his trap frequently, to which he follows up with another impatient remark.

Dylan or Rylie pipe up every so often to ask a random question. After several "I don't know" when they ask impossible questions, they move on to simpler inquiries. They want to know what we all do for fun and what daily life was like for us up until now.

To this, Scott glumly replies "The last two years have consisted of looking for *you* every day, so it hasn't been a walk through a candy store." He starts to say more, but my cutting glare silences him.

In an attempt to be polite, Jacklyn returns the question to Dylan and Rylie.

Rylie's description doesn't surprise us much. He lists off the weekly chores – scavenging for nearby supplies, tending to the livestock and crops, etc. When Dylan interrupts with details about weapon-making and training, enthusiasm rises.

"So, you guys trained every day for four years?" Jacklyn asks in disbelief.

"Yep," Dylan says as we climb over a fallen tree in our path. He watches me nervously as I jump onto the tree and proceed to leap off to the other side. Dylan hops the tree with only a hair less grace than me. We observe as the others must crawl up the trunk and awkwardly jump down. "Sometimes for four hours, sometimes longer. I guess it just depended on the day. Now, we only need to train a few times a week."

"What's your favorite part of training?"

"Well, I enjoyed archery and knife throwing. I would have to say my favorite was hand-to-hand combat, though. Rylie is our best offense, I'm an expert in defense, our friend Zavian is our best fighter in water, and Yuna is good with blades."

"Really?" I join the conversation. "Somehow I can't picture Yuna with sharp objects. I'd have to say my strong suits are knives and hand-to-hand. Jacklyn's a master with a blade."

"Well, that explains how you got that knife out of Rylie's hand so fast," says Dylan thoughtfully.

"Wait, he pulled a knife on you?" Scott asks in disbelief.

"Easy tiger," Jacklyn mutters and elbows Scott.

"Yeah," Rylie admits with a shrug. "Wouldn't 've been possible if she hadn't caught me off guard."

I roll my eyes. Dylan grins wickedly at his brother.

And Scott continues to glower.

"It was a misunderstanding!" Rylie exclaims. "I thought she was working for Cragen."

"And why would you think that?" Scott demands.

I hush them before anything else is said. "Shhhh…Listen…"

We're at the base of a steep hill. I hear faint gurgling sounds on the other side. I concentrate harder, straining my ears. There are several dull thumps in different times and pitches, drowned by the occasional loud *snap!*

I climb the hill, then proceed on all fours about halfway up. Scott and Dylan follow me on either side. We look out from behind tall grass to view the scene below.

There must be a dozen or more of them. Some make quiet snarls as they wander in circles, and the others chomp down on a dead horse – *where the hell did the horse come from?!* – and snap its bones to suck the marrow from inside. Scott makes an involuntary gagging noise. Dylan glowers at him. We retreat to warn the others.

"Is there any way to get around them?" Jacklyn wonders.

103

"Not without them hearing us," says Scott.

"Or smelling us," Dylan adds.

"Smelling us?" I ask.

"Their senses are heightened," Dylan explains. "They might be crazy because of the swelling in their brains, but they have advanced senses."

"Then let's just kill them and get it over with," Emmett says, withdrawing a dagger from his sheath.

I shrug. "Let's do it." I go to withdraw my weapon, too, then I realize I am unarmed. I do a quick scan, then make a made grab for the dagger on Scott's person.

"Hey! Give that back!" Scott whispers the demand, swiping for the blade. I jump back so he can't reach it. He groans, unsheathing his hunting knife.

"Maybe you should stay back," Dylan says quietly. I try to move around him. Dylan and Rylie block my path to the hill. Though he tries to be discreet as he repeats his whispered request, everyone notices, and all confused eyes are on me.

Okay, I *briefly* consider it. But this will go by much faster and with low casualties if I take the lead.

I snicker at them. "You know that's not gonna happen," I say, brushing between them to spearhead the group. "I've got this." They all rush to catch up with me.

I start down the other side of the hill. The infected must have heard us talking because they're plodding upward towards us. A tall, infected woman stagger towards me, blood of the horse oozing from her mouth with each snarl. I jump high enough to drive the blade down through her head. We drop.

I roll to the bottom of the hill, sweeping the legs on a chubby one. He falls on his back and throws his arms out to grab me. His browned fingernails sink into my side. I yelp out, shove my dagger through his open mouth.

I turn over just as a petite infected with a missing arm and matted black hair jumps on me. I throw my legs under her and shove. She flies over my head with a surprised growl. Before she can move, I summersault over the top of her and plant my blade into her skull. Her eyes grow wide. She releases one final snarl, then goes still.

I look to the others. They seem to be handling themselves just fine. It's over pretty fast! Almost all the infected are dead.

Except one.

Rylie has a buff-looking one cornered at a tree. The tree leans severely. It's mostly uprooted, clinging to the earth by a couple of thin roots. From the burn marks on the tilted trunk, I suspect lightning was the cause. It could give away at any time.

And it just had to be now.

Rylie stabs the infected through the chest, but that doesn't kill it. The infected staggers towards him, teeth bared. Rylie kicks the infected back into the tree and stabs again, this time through the temple. The pressure behind his drive is enough to break the tree free from the ground.

"Kaiya, move!" Scott yells.

As the nightmare predicted, the tree hurtles towards me. I don't have time to move. I squeeze my eyes shut and wait. *Let it be quick.*

Then someone shoves me hard in the back. I'm plunged to the ground just as the tree hits the forest floor with a vulgar *thud!* At that same moment, a familiar scream echo from behind.

"Oh god!" I scramble up and rush over to Dylan, pinned to the ground by the fallen tree. The giant trunk missed him – thank God! – but one of the thick branches traps his ankle.

"Gaahh!" he growls as he tried to pull himself free. The bough doesn't budge.

"Help me lift!" I holler. Emmett, Scott, and Rylie gather around the tree. I place my hands under the mass of bark. "One...two...three!" We lift the bough just high enough for Jacklyn to pull Dylan out. Once he's safely removed, we let it drop.

"Are you alright bro?" Rylie asks, searching Dylan over.

Dylan doesn't answer. He's making a strange noise from deep in his chest. It isn't until it grows louder that I realize he is *laughing*. Rylie grabs his brother's foot to remove his shoe. Dylan stops laughing and grinds his teeth together to suppress a yell.

"Are you insane?!" I demand, dropping to the ground beside them.

I give Dylan a quick look over. He still has all his limbs and digits. After determining that he is okay – aside from the clearly broken foot – I proceed to smack his arm.

"What the *hell* were you thinking?!"

"Be nice Kaiya," Scott scolds her. "He saved your life."

I shoot him the darkest of glares. *The one-time Scott takes his side…*

"Yeah Kaiya, be nice," Dylan mocks, then lets out another "*Ouch!*"

"You could have died, you idiot!"

"I didn't."

"But you *could* have!"

The others are spreading out to take watch for more infected who may have heard the commotion. Rylie and I tend to his wound. Rylie removes a first-aid kit from his bag slams it between us, rummaging through pill bottles.

Dylan looks up at me unapologetically, his brown eyes smoldering and pained.

"It was worth it."

"No, it wasn't," I growl through gritted teeth. I bow down to whisper in his ear. "You and I both know it won't make a difference. Next time, just let it happen."

At first, he looks shocked and muddled. Then, understanding lights across his face. He laughs again, this time quiet and confident. "–T's not gonna happen."

I want to make an angry retort, but I bite my tongue. I can scream at him more about it later. Rylie withdraws a small pill bottle from the bag. The bottle reads *oxycodone* for a Susan Stone, but that can't be what the pills are. These capsules are purple and speckled. He pours two small capsules into my hand, then replaces the cap. "This," Rylie holds one up to Dylan, "is like a strong pain killer. We made it in the lab. It will numb the pain *and* heal your injury within twenty-four hours. Don't worry, it's safe. I've taken it

107

myself. But…we will need to realign your ankle and the bones in your foot, or they will reform crooked. Do you understand?"

Where the hell were these pills I needed them?!

Dylan bites his lip hard, and nods. "Do it."

I give him the pills, as Rylie instructs, and holler for Jacklyn. She crouches down over Dylan to inspect his injured foot. She gives him an apologetic glance and grabs the foot, feeling around the bones with her thumb. Rylie quickly puts the strap from his backpack between Dylan's teeth, so he won't scream or bite off his tongue.

"I think it's fractured in a few places. That's good; we won't need to push any bones back into place. His ankle, however,…" she turns it over in her hand, making Dylan squirm. My hand itches to smack her arm for making him wriggle this way, so I step back. Dylan lets out a stifled cry. "I think it's dislocated. The tendons and ligaments don't feel like they're torn, but I can't be sure…I think I can pop it back in. Even if it doesn't go in all the way, it should heal after the medicine kicks in." Jacklyn looks from me to Rylie. "Should I…?"

"Do it," Rylie says on his brother's behalf.

Jacklyn strips off her jacket and rolls it up, placing it under Dylan's knee. "I'm going to need you to hold his leg down," she says, and reaches up to position Rylie's hands – one on his thigh and the other on the side of his shin. She then positions herself, so her knee is on the ground up against the opposite side of his shin, her hands on his foot.

"Ready?"

Dylan nods. I kneel forward, grab his hand, and squeezed it gently.

Pop!

The strap doesn't stifle his agonizing howl.

I cringe.

Damn it and damn *him*! I was supposed to be the one smashed by that tree! Who the hell hops in the line of fire for someone they don't even know?

Chapter 10

After about thirty minutes of fashioning a splint for his foot out of a couple of sticks and a ripped t-shirt from one of the infected, we set off again. Rylie and I wrap our arms around Dylan to guide him through the forest. Scott walks in front of us to help him across dips in the ground, while Jacklyn and Emmett scout about a hundred-fifty or so yards ahead to find somewhere we can lay low so Dylan can recover. My eyes sweep the forest at every noise. Last thing we need is a horde sneaking up on us.

Rylie accidentally bumps Dylan's splint as we carry him up a small incline.

"Sorry, sorry," Rylie apologizes.

"Don't be," I say. "He's an idiot. He did it to himself."

"What was I supposed to do?" Dylan wonders through gritted teeth.

"Let nature take its course," I say. "And stay away from falling trees!"

"I wasn't just going to let it *crush you*," he says and rolls his eyes, as if the very idea is trivial. Perhaps it is, but I refuse to see his behavior and damaged foot as chivalry. "Besides, a broken foot is a lot easier to deal with than a broken skull."

I shake my head. "You've just delayed the inevitable."

"We don't know that," Dylan defends. "By the way...how did you know?"

"I overheard you two talking last night," I say.

"So, you know about the dream?" Rylie wonders.

"Yeah, I do. But we can discuss it later."

"Yes, let's," Dylan agrees.

The remainder of our walk is silent. We walk like this for almost a couple hours and stop every so often to let Dylan rest.

Since we're taking care of Dylan, I don't have time to worry about my own injury. It isn't until we've been walking for over an hour that I notice the sting in my side. I lean up against a sturdy tree – yes, I double check *this* tree first – and pull my shirt up to inspect it.

The four gashes are shallow and long, but nothing major. The side of my shirt – or, rather, Dylan's shirt – is drenched in blood. Luckily, no one has noticed yet. I can only fathom how Scott would react if he paid attention. With a sigh, I realize I need the first-aid kit and another set of hands.

"Jacklyn, can you help me with this?" I call to her. She's seated in the dirt with Emmett just a few yards from me. She jumps delicately to her feet and skips over only to skid to a stop when she sees my wound.

"What is that?!" she demands, pointing at my side.

"Shh!" Everyone looks at me again. Figures. I try to avoid attention as much as humanly possible, but I have eyes pulled to me on a regular basis (no thanks to

111

Scott and Jacklyn with their frequent outbursts of raw emotion).

"It's just a scratch," I say. "Can you help me wrap it?"

"Well, you need to clean it first," she gripes, back-tracking to Rylie's bag for the first-aid kit.

"Did one of the infected do this to you?" Scott asks from beside Rylie. They're seated on a flat-topped boulder wedged into the side of a small hill.

"Yeah, but it's nothing. No need to be concerned about it."

Scott grumbles something unintelligible to Dylan and Rylie. Dylan *mhmm*'s, Rylie snickers.

Once Jacklyn's done fussing over my scratch, I ask her to discreetly check my mark. She traces up my neck with one finger, parting into my hair. Jacklyn's finger rests on the mark's new height. I shiver. It's moved again. She doesn't say anything, giving my shoulders a gentle squeeze before she moves over to check Dylan's bandages. I don't want to be in the way, so I sit cross-legged on the ground, back to the tree.

Once my butt is planted, I realize how rundown I am. My body is like gelatin and my side throbs. I take a deep breath and try to relax for a moment before we start walking again, but the fatigue drowns me.

Relaxing proves to be difficult. I feel two sets of eyes on me. Out of the corner of my eye I catch Rylie and Dylan staring intently, whispering back and forth. Too tired to eavesdrop on their conversation, I close my eyes. Narrowly escaping death is exhausting!

The memory of Dylan jumping in the line of the tree suddenly demands my attention. I still can't understand it. I'm a stranger to him. And now I owe him. *Great*. Though I'm annoyed with him and his chivalrous attitude, I have to admit that he intrigues me. There are so many questions to ask him. Does he get a kick out of near-death experiences? But other less snarky questions press on the back of my mind. Questions like 'How the hell have you and your brother survived up until now?' because surely his sense of danger hasn't done him any favors, and 'What's it like running your own community?' Inevitably, there are more personal questions. Things only to be revealed to a close confidant.

Can I be his confidant? His friend? His ally? More?

This mission to get answers from Cragen while keeping Dylan alive serves as a great excuse to get to know him. To get answers. To give myself closure – or, at least, that's what I'm telling myself. I'm going to enjoy it while I can – you know before I die.

****

We give up on walking through the trees since the mongril's tracks have unexpectantly ended – did they cover their tracks? Did their footsteps in the dirt magically disappear after only a few hours? Or am I so absorbed in my own thoughts that I lost the ability to follow basic trails? – so Rylie leads us to the highway. Dylan and Rylie are the only two who've successfully escaped Cragen's compound, so they outline the quickest path on the map while we look for a place we can camp out. It's difficult to read the map while walking, so we stop for a while. I spread it out on the hood of one of the abandoned cars on the shoulder of the road. We all huddle around it.

It's getting late. We can't stay out in the open during the night. After the horde of infected and the noise from the fallen tree, it was best not to risk sleeping in the tents tonight. There's an old *Quality Inn* hotel half a mile from the highway. I think that might be a good place to crash.

"The hotel is right off this exit," I trace the line on the map, then point at the ramp ahead of us. "It's easy to get to and it's not too far off course."

"But wouldn't it have been a high-traffic place before the disaster?" Emmett asks. "That place could be swarming with infected for all we know."

"Do you have a better idea?"

"I don't think it would be," Rylie shakes his head. "It wasn't a particularly popular place to stay back in the day. Plus, it's a fairly small hotel."

"It's settled then."

Breaking into the hotel is child's play. This *Quality Inn* had no sliding doors. The glass double doors have an old school lock easily picked with a bobby pin. If they had an alarm system, it must not be active anymore. Must not have had enough money for renovations.

Though deserted, it appears to be in good shape. The furniture shows no wear or tear. The beige walls have only slightly yellowed. Outdated maroon décor remains untouched. Everything is tidy, aside from thick layers of dust on the hard surfaces. I suggest we all sleep in the lobby area, just to be on the safe side. Everyone agrees. Jacklyn and Emmett gather all the beds and sofas they find on the first floor and bring them out to the spacious lobby, so we all have comfortable sleeping arrangements. I flop onto one of

114

the mattresses. It's luxuriously soft. Well, in comparison to what I've slept on the last two and a half years, at least. I probably could have fell asleep then and there, but I don't quite feel comfortable sleeping in this place without giving it a brief search. I excuse myself as the others form the beds and sofas into a circle with all our supplies in the center for protection.

It doesn't take long to search the first floor. The bedroom doors remain open from the mattress raid. I check all closets and bathrooms for supplies – or on the off chance, an infected. Nothing but extra blankets and sheets.

I proceed up the stairwell to the second floor. All these doors are locked. Since I don't have a keycard, I have to break into them (not like a keycard would work, anyways. There's no power and any battery-operated doors would be dead by now). I kick in the first door and withdraw my dagger. Searching the room takes thirty seconds. Nothing.

I sigh and plop myself down in the recliner.

So, this is what staying in a hotel feels like. It's nice.

My body seems to melt into the cushions. I wish I could relax and stay here for a few hours. I sigh yet again. I will never know what it feels like to relax. I'm always on guard. Always alert. Always waiting for one of my nightmares to appear in front of me. For Dylan to die in some freak accident, one I've foreseen but still cannot control. Always waiting for the other shoe to drop.

I don't remember feeling tired enough to fall asleep.

But here I am, stuck in another night terror.

115

Dylan's beside me in a white room, one I'm starting to become familiar with. We're backed up against a gurney on the only open wall.

Growls and claws on wood sound from the door. Three or more distorted faces fight for space in the small window.

"Shit!" Dylan says, eyes searching frantically for an exit.

But there is none. We're trapped, alone in this strangely bright room.

The door trembles, the shakes grow more and more forceful, until finally the wood frame breaks free, and they pour in.

"Shit!" he says again. He shoves the gurney aside, pushes me against the wall, then flips the gurney to block me into a corner.

"Come on!" I try to pull him behind the makeshift barricade.

But my arms won't work.

The infected pull him into a circular swarm. They chomp delightedly on his flesh as he screams.

Thump.

I rip myself off the chair and walk towards the door.

I stop just shy of the doorframe. Something is coming up the stairway. *Thump, click. Thump, click.* Blade poised, round the corner…

And nearly knock over Dylan.

"Jesus!" I exclaim, shoving the dagger back into its sheath. "You scared me."

"Sorry," he laughs. He looks flustered from the walk.

"Where did you get the cane?"

"Scott found it hanging on a coat rack. Cool, right?"

"Right. Umm…what are you doing up here? You should be resting."

Dylan grimaces. I've never seen him grimace before. It looks foreign on his cheeks. "I figured you were going to yell at me about the tree, so I came up here so you could do it without an audience. So, go ahead."

I cross my arms and glare at him. He appears exhausted, purple rings adding an aged look to his red eyes. I lean up against the wall. "Some of it makes sense now. I see why you did it, but I don't get why you would hurt yourself in the process – or why you even care, for that matter. So…that's why you came after me? To make sure I don't die?"

"Yeah, kinda," he admits. He leans against the wall, too.

"Look," I say, looking away from him to stare at the red carpet. "You don't have to protect me. I can protect myself. Even if I did die, it wouldn't be your fault. You wouldn't have my blood on your hands."

He stares me down now. "You think I'm doing this out of guilt? Because I don't want blood on my hands?"

I look up at him with confusion. "That's what you said to Rylie. Aren't you?"

"No," he says like it is obvious. "I just don't want you to die."

"…Why?"

Dylan sighs and slides down to the floor, extending his leg so his injured foot blocks access to the hall.

"I don't know, honestly. Sorry if that sounds rude. But I don't know why I care. I shouldn't, but I do. I get this…vibe, that you're too important to die."

"And is that why you suggested we stay with you?"

"Maybe."

"But why…with the tree…?" I can't seem to find the right words to phrase my question.

It's quiet for a minute. Dylan twiddles his thumbs. Then, gawking at his hands, he breaks the short silence.

"It's strange. It was just like every other nightmare I've told you about, yet different. I would try to warn you, but I couldn't talk. And you would scream for me. You didn't know me, I didn't know you, and yet you would scream my name like I was the only person who could help you. Then the tree would crush you, and I'd watch you die, just like every other time. But it was different. More realistic. Like I could feel the weight of the tree crushing my chest, as well. Then I had that nightmare about the mongrils taking you, and it actually happened, minus the stabbing. So, when I saw the tree falling, for *real* this time, I…" he trails off.

"And so, you figured that you could just take my place?'

He nods. "I couldn't in the dream, so maybe I could stop it in real life."

"Then what makes you think that pushing me out of the way and taking my place in real life would work?"

"It did, didn't it? You're still alive."

"For now."

"Why do you think I'm having these dreams about you?" Dylan asks abruptly. He turns his body to face me.

"I'm not sure," I say. He looks disappointed with my answer. His eyes sink to the floor. "But it's not your job to keep me alive. We should be more worried about Cragen and the mongrils."

Just as Dylan opens his mouth to speak, a clambering and groaning from the opposite stairwell interrupts us. I jump upright. Sounds like infected trapped behind the door. I pull Dylan to his feet.

"I'm going to check it out," I tell him in a hushed voice. "Go downstairs and warn the others."

Dylan glares.

I groan. "Okay, fine! Just stay put."

I walk towards the silver stairwell door cautiously. The wired window in the door displays the steps, but I don't see anything else. I inch closer and put my face against the glass to get a better look. Nothing on this floor. Nothing on the stairs leading up.

But on the stairs leading down to the first floor, there must be more than twenty infected crammed together. Some of them are pressed up against the door leading out to the lobby hall. It's like a scary mosh pit! I wonder how long it will be before the infected realize they can open that door...

I half-jog back to Dylan. "We have to go, now!" I grab hold of his side and tow him towards the stairs.

"How many?"

I try to keep his foot from hitting the stairs as we take them three at a time. "Enough that we need to get out of here," I answer.

Once we reach the bottom of the stairs, I release Dylan and run forward.

"Guys! We have a problem!" I exclaim. The men stop laughing and turn to look at me, concerned. But one person is missing.

"Where's Jacklyn?"

Scott frowns. "Doing her rounds. She went to check the other stairwell."

Oh, no.

My heart does a frightened flip as I sprint down the hallway to the stairwell. Jacklyn's almost to the door, but she hasn't noticed the infected behind it. She gawks at the generic paintings on the left wall as she walks.

"Jacklyn, stop!" I yell.

She pivots on her heel and raises her arms in question.

"What? I'm just going to do a quick sweep."

I point behind her. "Look at the door."

She turns slowly and freezes when she sees the distorted faces staring back at her from the small window. The infected snarl loudly now, clawing at the door and window with their long, crooked nails. They're trying desperately to get to her. To us. To the lobby full of walking meals.

"We need to grab our bags and go," I say. I close the distance between us in four long strides and grab her arm.

She nods, not looking away from the wire window. "At least they can't open doo –"

The door flies open. The first four infected topple to the floor. The rest trample over the fallen and lurch at us.

"Or maybe they can!" We sprint back up the hall and shout.

"Get out! GO NOW!" I scream at them. The hall opens into the lobby. The gang frantically throws bags on their backs.

"Forget the stuff and go!" Jacklyn yells, grabbing hold of Emmett and heading for the door. She pauses long enough to snatch the bag with the first-aid kit, which she has placed strategically on the bed she claimed.

I whip out my blade and twist around. Just in time to slice the throat of an infected. Blood splatters my face and it collapses at my feet.

"Scott!" I reach for a blade on the nearest bed and fling it at Scott, who stands in the center trying to grab bags. He catches the hilt of the dagger and leaps over the bed to assist me.

I do a two-second scan of the room. Jacklyn and Emmett are outside. Rylie and Dylan aren't. *Naturally*. Rylie, with a bag on his back, tries to help Dylan towards the door, but he won't budge.

Dylan hollers at me to come on. He tries to limp towards me – towards the horde – but his brother restrains him.

I look over at Scott. He decapitates a short and stout infected woman. "Get them out of here, I will hold them off!"

"Not a chance," he says, swinging the blade at another. The infected dodges his blow, and swats at him. Scott recoils. I kick the infected in the chest. It tumbles back.

I shove Scott towards the door with my free hand. "I'm not asking. Get them out. I'm right behind you." I stab one through the chest, and another in the temple.

Scott stands there for a split second, watching me. "Be careful." Then he runs over to Dylan and scoops him up like a toddler. "Go!" he yells at Rylie. Rylie flies towards the exit. Scott follows, Dylan thrashing violently in his arms.

"Kaiya! You idiot!" Dylan protests as they exit the building. I back towards the doors myself.

I swing my blade in front of me. Two grey arms drop to the floor. Another step back, another swipe of my blade. This time a head pops off. More blood hits my face.

I'm gonna need a wash after this. Another step back. Kick one backwards. Slash at another. Nails claw at my arm. Swing! No more hand. More nails at my side, ripping open my previous wound. *AHH!* Dagger to the heart. More angry howls.

"Get out of there!" Scott's muffled cry echoes through the door.

I take another step back, and chance a look over my shoulder. Seven feet from the doors. The others watch me nervously from the parking lot. Rylie holds Dylan's arms behind his back while Scott blocks his path. They're closest to the doors. Scott looks like he's debating to run back in to aid me.

I turn back to the assailants. They swarm around me. One is so close it grabs my arm and pulls me in, sinking its teeth into my neck. I yelp and twist the dagger into the belly of the infected. The jaw drags with my movement, elongating the wound before the infected drops. Luckily, the bite isn't too deep. Blood flows evenly from it. No gushing. But the surge of hot fluid is enough to crescendo their growls. Crazed wide eyes dive for me.

This is my only chance. I spin towards the door and run for it.

Sharp nails claw at my back. I cry out in pain. Thank heavens they aren't smart enough to grab me by my ankles as I dive through the doorway.

I skid onto the cement, dropping my blade. The pavement scrapes a layer of my skin from my cheek and elbows. The jean fabric rips at my knees.

Scott's swiftly in front of me. He pulls the doors to the hotel shut, locking the monsters inside. I throw him my dagger from the ground. He catches it effortlessly and jams it through the handles.

I gasp with relief and lay my head back, ignoring the stinging sensation that covers my entire body. The normalized sting in my back is now an ever-present burn. I don't have to look to know what's happened.

"*Phew*! There. They aren't getting out now," Scott says.

I'm still on the ground, breathing heavily. When I sit up, my eyes go directly to the door, where the infected pound on the glass and snarl at us, at *me*. I notice then that one of them had torn my shirt. A scrap of green cloth is stuck to a talon of the infected as it continues to scratch at the glass.

"You alright?" Dylan asks. I look up and wince against the twinge in my neck. Dylan and Rylie tower over me.

"Just peachy," I laugh, though it sounds more like a *huff* than a laugh. Dylan backs away to give me breathing room, muttering about how I *must be crazy* under his breath. I stand slowly in front of the others. "Is everyone okay?"

Of course, they're all staring at me in shock. No one says anything. I still breathe heavily. I lean over to put my hands on my knees, taking deep gulps of air. Each breathe burns a little. Surely not from overexertion. Perhaps it's a side-affect from the mixture of fear and adrenaline.

There's a clearing of throat, followed by a gruff *ach-hem*.

Two gentlemen stand ten yards behind Jacklyn and Emmett.

How did we not hear them approach? Too wrapped up in my latest near-death experience, I suppose.

Instinctively, we jump into a defensive line. We point our weapons at the intruders – well, aside from me...my weapon is still being used as a handle wedge on the doors – just as the bigger one steps forward. He stops after four or five feet. His dark eyes narrow on me.

"Kaiya?"

Chapter 11

"Kaiya, you're alive?" The man steps forward. We all stiffen at the movement.

He freezes, arms up.

"Who are you?" Scott asks.

The man ignores him, eyes still pasted to me. "Kaiya, don't you remember me?"

All eyes shift to me.

The man waits patiently. He's large with linebacker shoulders and a dark buzzcut. His beard is scraggly and patchy, the colors that of a brown calico. Something about the dip in his temples and his stacked cheekbones reminds me of a time long before all this – a time I feel I'm not supposed to remember. Before I woke up two years ago, before I made a family with Scott and Jacklyn and Emmett...

And a distant memory forces its way to the front. I'm temporarily blinded by it.

All I can see is this man. But he's younger. Shorter. Same shape and cheekbones. He's laughing over something...a bad joke? Yeah, he told horrendous jokes. We watch a slasher film together, then anime, then a raunchy comedy with some skinny blonde he obsesses over the whole one-hundred-and-twenty-three minutes. *She's so pretty*, he's saying. *It would take the end of the world for me to find someone with sweet eyes like that.*

But who is he? Why are we laughing so much? Is he the man who taught me to punch? Yeah, I remember! My mean right hook left his eye purple and swollen for weeks. And on picture day! I even tried to cover it with foundation. He wasn't happy about that. And neither were the other freshmen boys. I'm suddenly outside the senior chem room, telling him that boys are mean, and they will be like that until the world forces them to grow up.

And then a darker moment in time, one that leaves me in regret as I recall. I suppress the memory, but his yelling still rings in the deepest corners. As it all fades, I remember yelling his name, but his figure retreats into blackness.

I blink rapidly, pulling back to the now.

"Barris?" I say.

He grins widely. "Yes, that's right! It's cousin Barris."

A nervous laugh escapes my lips. Always making me laugh, you son of a bitch.

I step towards my cousin, but a warm hand shocks my elbow with a tight grip.

"You know him?" Dylan asks in a low voice.

"Yeah. I remember him," I say. Though he doesn't look convinced, his grip eases. "I don't know how, but I remember him. Just him."

After a second, Dylan gives a wavering nod and releases me. I look to the others and repeat the confirmation.

"It's okay, he's my cousin. I remember him."

And then I give Barris the reunion bear-hug he deserves.

"I thought you were dead!" he exclaims, his voice giddy. "But here you are, scrawny and pasty as ever!"

"And here you are…and you have a beard!"

The other man – I almost forgot about him! – clears his throat again.

"You going to introduce me?" he asks. He has a high voice for a man, thick with annoyance.

Barris spins me to face his friend, a walking toothpick! *And he called me scrawny.* Dirty blonde hair, dark complexion, and a couple crooked black teeth to match his sideways smile.

"Kaiya, this is Kade. I've been traveling with him for the last three years." Barris steps between us, gesturing introductions with his beefy hands. "Kade, this is my older cousin Kaiya."

Kade waves shyly, though he doesn't seem to be a shy guy. He glances at the others.

"Where have you been all this time?" Barris asks.

"It's a long story," I say. Where do I even begin? And I can't tell it here. Not with that nightmare of a hotel still looming over me.

"It's nearly sunset. We should find a place to sleep, and soon," Rylie says.

"Do we really want to chance staying in another building?" Scott asks, looking around. "I mean, they could all be swarmed for all we know."

"He's right," Jacklyn agrees. She's visibly shaken. "Where are we going to go for the night?"

"We'll go back to the forest," I say. "We'll just have to take turns on watch, two people at a time." I turn my attention back to Barris and Kade for a moment. "You guys are welcome to join. We can talk more once we set up camp."

Dylan clears his throat behind me, then changes the subject when I turn to glare at him.

"How much of the supplies did we save?" Dylan wonders. Everyone puts their packs down on the pavement and empties them.

I step forward to join the circle around the supplies, ignoring the eager snarls from the glass behind us. Not an easy feat, mind you. Each snarl begs me to get as far from here as possible.

After taking inventory, we discover that we're missing two bags. We're low on food – but not so low that we need to worry. We're missing a few guns and other weapons, some clothes, and first aid bandages. Only four of the six tents they brought from the community were rescued. *Great.* Kade suggests that we go back in, kill the infected, and retrieve our supplies. He quickly rethinks as we all frown at him.

We leave the hotel. Even walking past the highway and into the trees, I swear I can still hear their vicious growls and claws on glass. I let Rylie lead the way through the forest. I hang towards the back, trying to straighten my head out. I can't get the growls and screams out of my head.

Scott walks protectively behind me, but he keeps his distance. I think he knows I'm struggling to get a grip. Dylan walks up towards the front with Emmett and Jacklyn, who chat up Barris and Kade. Emmett helps Dylan through the uneven ruts in the forest floor.

Rylie finally stops us in a small meadow. From the meadow, we can no longer see the road. Perfect! It'll be more difficult to be found here. As they frantically set up camp under the setting sun and my cousin is engaged in conversation with Scott, I excuse myself to gather some firewood.

Thankfully, no one follows me this time. I'm alone.

I found an armful of twigs and fallen branches. I'm prepared to head back, but then I spot more firewood by a small creek. I sit on the bank, kick off my shoes and stick my toes in the cold water. The disruptive ripple breaks through the calm water as crickets chirp on the other side of the bank.

How can such a peaceful place like this survive in such a cruel and disgusting world? Right beside the gentle water and quiet bugs coincides the snarling beasts, literal nightmares and a supposedly sadistic Cragen. How can two complete opposites be found only a mile apart?

I sigh, and plant my feet firmly in the water, mud mushing between my toes. The water comes up to my shin. I don't care that my pantlegs are getting wet. I bend over and cup my hands under the water. It's chilly and refreshing on my calloused skin. I raise the water to my face and wash off the smeared blood. The unsanitary water prickles my exposed dermis.

For the brief moment my eyes are closed, I'm pulled back in the hotel with infected closing around me. I gasp and rub my eyes, but the image won't disappear. Claws at my arms, teeth bared at my neck…it's like a nightmare that won't end. I rapidly splash my face with the creek water to help me focus.

I stand in the creek for what feels like forever. I want desperately for the nightmare to end. *Try thinking of something different.* But the only other thing on my mind is my dream about Dylan. *That* is something I need to confront, as well.

Protecting Dylan won't be the hard part – that is, as long as he doesn't do anything stupid. But guarding him while staying on guard with myself will prove to be challenging. How the hell am I going to protect Dylan from getting himself killed AND keep myself alive? How do I protect him from me? I'm sure I can enlist Jacklyn's help if I need to, but I don't want her in harm's way, either. Or maybe telling Dylan about my worst nightmare will keep him away from me, and then his blood won't be on my hands…

No, I can't do that. I *need* to be where he is. My stomach twists at the thought of something happening to him.

Twigs crunch behind me.

"Easy, it's just me," Scott steps into the creek, palms forward in defense.

"Hi," I say. I go back to washing blood from my arms.

"You've got a little something…" Scott wades in closer to me and points to his cheek, "right there."

"Ha-ha, real funny."

Scott closes the distance between us, a strange longing evident in his eyes as he wipes the bloody spot I missed.

"Thanks," I say, flashing him a grimace. I bet my smile is more of a scared-shitless grimace. He places an oversized hand over the cheek. It burns my scrapes.

"You okay?"

I just nod.

"Little more danger than you wanted today?" he guesses.

Again, I can only nod.

Scott pulls me into a bear hug. My joints complain, but I don't refuse. In fact, I welcome the nerve-crushing warmth. Normally, I shy away from physical contact, or any sort of comfort, really. But this is different somehow. This isn't like the passes Scott has made on me in the past. This is a different sort of longing, one that doesn't involve lip-locks. The way a person longs to wipe away the tears of a hurt friend.

"Thank you," I say as I nuzzle into his shoulder. He really is like a big teddy bear.

Scott looks down at me. "Anytime."

A comfortable moment passes like this.

Then something else creeps in.

Dylan's hug was just as comforting, if not more, when he rescued me from Blair and the mongrils. It only lasted a few seconds at most, but his arms were warm and crushing around me. I remember thinking that was not the right time to hug, but maybe it was. Maybe it's just what I needed in that moment, even if I thought he was stupid.

So why am I thinking about this *now*? In Scott's arms?

But two voices interrupt my internal dialogue.

I jump back from Scott and look up to see Barris and Dylan on the bank. Barris clears his throat

131

theatrically, a smug grin pointed at me. No doubt what's going through his mind. But it's Dylan's expression I care about. A delicate crease forms between his brows and his mouth parts in surprise. Or is it jealousy?

Is Dylan protecting me because he cares for me?

Wait…do *I* care for *him*?

"So, this is where you ran off to," Barris says. He crosses his arms, grin widening.

I frown at my cousin, flashing a look to Dylan. "I had to wash the infected blood off."

But Dylan avoids me completely, his eyes on Scott.

"Rylie's got the first aid kit handy," Dylan says, a certain roughness layering his voice. "You should probably have your wounds cleaned and dressed."

"And we should probably talk," Barris adds. "There's a lot to tell you."

"Right." Scott and I make our way to the bank. Scott grabs my pile of firewood and takes off ahead of us.

I sit on the ground and ring the water from my pantlegs. Dylan holds out a fresh linen. Must have gotten it from the hotel.

"You good?" I ask, dabbing myself dry.

He shrugs. Not very convincing. "Why wouldn't I be?" No, not convincing at all. His sideways glances give it away.

"Look, that wasn't–"

But he cuts me off. "Are *you* alright?"

"I'm fine," I say, watching Barris follow Scott's path back to camp. It's just Dylan and I out here. It's nearly dark out now, and the hotel memory seems to be locked up for the moment. "I just needed a minute alone. You understand."

"Sure, sure," he says, rubbing his shoulder. "Alone. I get it."

I groan. "I *was* alone, until Scott showed up! He's just being a good friend."

Dylan considers that for a moment, then mutters *good friend* under his breath. He sighs quietly and shrugs again, as if trying to convince himself what I say is true. "Come on," he pushes me towards the camp. "You need to dry off, and I need to doctor you up."

"I can take care of myself; you know."

"True, but I wouldn't be a very good *friend* if I didn't help out."

Insert internal groan here. Dylan's just as oblivious as I am. He can't admit that he cares for me on a strangely richer level.

For that matter, neither can I.

Chapter 12

"It all happened a few years ago, more or less, but it's hard to keep track of the years as they creep by."

After a few minutes of talking about our family, Barris finally launches into the story of how they died, how he escaped Cragen, and how I disappeared. We're all gathered in the center of our tent circle, Dylan, Barris and I closest to the fire so I can warm up. Dylan helps me clean the marks on my shoulder and my sides as Barris talks. The others lean forward, listening intently.

"You'd been missing for three days when we decided we couldn't wait for the police to find you," he says, staring into the dancing flames. "I just knew your disappearance had something to do with the missing teens. They were being taken for this 'study.' But it didn't matter. The infected had already swarmed most the state. Anyway, they told everyone to evacuate before the infected would reach this area, but your family refused to leave. They wanted to find you first.

"We found their bodies a week later, just before things got worse. My mom was devastated. She was determined to find you, for her sister, but things got so hectic that we had no choice but to flee. We stopped by the penitentiary first."

"Why?" I ask. "You thought I was there?"

"No," he says slowly. "But your sister had been there for about a year before the radiation."

I raise a brow at him. "I had a sister?"

"May still have," Barris corrects. "We never found her. The penitentiary was abandoned. Many of its…inhabitants…were left behind."

A sister. I had a sister.

"What did she look like?"

"Bianca had the same facial features as you, but you could tell by her eyes that she was a younger sibling. She had brown hair and eyes as dark as an abyss."

"What was she locked up for?" Rylie asks from his place behind his brother. I shoot him a murderous glare, to which he rolls his eyes. Typical.

"Nothing. A misunderstanding, really. He said, she said. Yatta."

"It's just weird. I never really considered the possibility that I'd have living relatives in this mess. Yet, here you are," I gesture a shaking hand at Barris. "Quite possibly my last living relative. A real blast from the past…well, what small pieces I can remember."

He looks down at his hands for a moment, then back at me, his eyes a brighter blaze than the fire next to us. "Perhaps…but the past has a way of biting you in the ass."

They change the subject. Rylie rudely inquires about Barris and Kade's adventures up to now, which

135

spurs a new chat about infected. I don't pay much attention to the conversation. It just sounds like garbled gibberish against the crackling wood and the ringing in my head.

As always, I feel a pair of eyes on me. I don't look around the campfire to find whom they belong to, though I have a pretty good guess. I know he's pissed that I stayed behind to fight off the infected, *and* that Scott and I shared a moment in the creek. The stare pushes on me like a ton of bricks.

Everyone turns in relatively early. Emmett and I take the first watch while the others sleep. It's mostly quiet. We just sit in front of the campfire and stare off into the woods. Emmett shifts uncomfortably on the log every few seconds. I strain not to do the same. Don't want to add to the discomfort.

Don't get me wrong. It's only uncomfortable because I've never been alone with Emmett for this long. He's usually accompanied by Jacklyn, or I'm accompanied by Scott. And as if this isn't odd enough, I can sense skepticism in every glance he grants me. What's his problem?

Emmett clears his throat after ten more minutes of awkward silence.

"How are you feeling?"

I hike up my shirt to look at the marks on my side. They're nothing but tiny papercuts now. No doubt the ones on my back look the same.

"Pretty good," I say. "Fast healer, remember?"

"Right," Emmett murmurs. He stretches dramatically. "So…you dig dream boy?"

I groan loudly and curse again. "Stop it."

"Stop what?" he says innocently, but his grin grows devilish.

"Just stop talking." Why does he have to do this now? And why Emmett?

"Fine. But you can't avoid it forever, you know." He takes a long stick from our dwindling firewood pile and starts poking at the embers. I see him flashing me a *let's talk about it* look from the corner of his eye.

I groan again. "You are infuriating, you know that?"

"I know," he says proudly. "Jacklyn says it all the time."

I punch his shoulder a little harder than intend. "I don't 'dig' Dylan."

"So, you just like him?"

My cheeks burn.

"I…care about him not dying. That's all."

"Really?"

"Yes, really," I say, but the squeaky tone in my voice betrays me. "And if Scott heard us talking about this, he would–"

"He wouldn't do anything," Emmett says firmly. He narrows his already squinty eyes at me, the green ablaze. "He knows this is as far as your relationship will ever go. He's fine in the friend-zone."

"Which one's in the friend-zone?" A voice asks, making us jump. We both turn to find Barris crawling out of his tent.

"What are you doing up?" I ask.

He sits cross-legged beside me in the dirt.

"I was eavesdropping. It's fun. You should try it sometime."

Emmett snickers, still prodding the fire.

"What's the big deal?" Barris continues with a friendly smile. "You like Scott."

"What? No!"

"Scott's the one in the friend-zone," Emmett explains.

"Ah. So, you like *Dylan*," He says with confusion in his eyes. "So what?"

So what? So what? It's Dylan. We're both on Death's list. Even if I did like him, it would never work. It would only end in pain.

But *do* I like him?

I think about him now, my mind so wrapped up in the idea of him liking me, analyzing every look, every word shared, every possibly intimate moment. Just the image of his bright brown eyes burning through me heats my face. Okay, maybe I do care about him the way he cares for me…the way he won't admit…

There's no point in denying it any longer. Barris and Emmett are the most stubborn men I have ever had the pleasure of knowing, besides Scott. They will keep poking at me until I cave. So, I decide to skip the poking stage and get straight to ripping the bandage.

"Okay, let's say I do." I keep my voice low so no one will overhear. "But I'm not supposed to. I mean, I've known the guy for…a week maybe?" I'm having trouble keeping track of the time that's passed. "He'd think I'm crazy. And what about Scott? He's my best friend. I can't do that to him."

"Give Scott some credit," Emmett says, patting my shoulder blade. He means well, but it's hard to be comforted when pushed forward by a slap on the back. I don't think he realizes how much force he's using. "He isn't pressuring you into anything. And he knows how you feel about him…and how you feel about this guy."

"He does? How?"

"Oh, puh-lease," he says in the most effeminate voice he can muster. "He isn't stupid. It's pretty obvious. I've only just met everyone and it's obvious."

"It is?"

"Just the way you look at him says it all," says Emmett.

I grunt at them. "Just cut it out, both of you. I'm not telling him, if that's what you guys are getting at. We need to focus on the mission. And on keeping Rylie and Dylan out of trouble."

"Gotcha," Barris says, jumping to his feet. "I've got next shift, so why don't you go get some sleep."

"I don't want sleep."

"Afraid you'll have nightmares?" Emmett asks casually. Again, he sees right through me.

"It's stupid, but I know I'll dream about that hotel if I do go to sleep."

A half-truth, but a fear non the less. Between my thoughts of Dylan and the questions bubbling up for Barris, there is no way I can sleep. Not yet.

Emmett shrugs. "Well, try to get rest at some point. I have a feeling there's more excitement to come tomorrow."

I grimace. It's a pity Emmett and I don't talk more often. He's a good friend. "Thanks."

Emmett disappears into Jacklyn's tent. Barris and I are finally alone.

"I know you're going to ask about *him*," Barris says. He avoids my questioning gaze as he speaks.

"And it's not going to be a pleasant conversation, so let's get it over with."

I gulp, hand trembling as I reach into my pocket to retrieve the picture I took from Rylie and Dylan days before. I've held it close to me until I could get answers, and the time has come for some of the mystery to disappear. My gut twists violently as my mind races. I have theories about *him*, but part of me wants to keep my blissful ignorance.

I hand him the picture of Cragen holding me.

"Tell me about him. How did we know each other?"

Flames reflect in Barris' irises, remorse dancing behind them.

"Cragen was your best friend," he says quietly. "He was a good friend of mine, too, until you two had it out."

"What do you mean?"

"It was funny then, but now it's sort of sick to think about. I was convinced he was your perfect match. You two did everything together. He went to all your volleyball matches, he took Kenpo classes with you, he took punches for you, he even went out to buy feminine products for you. The guy was head over heels. Cragen just got his master's degree and planned to get his doctorate in biochemistry just like his parents, and at such a young age. You'd just started teaching at the local high school."

"So, what happened?"

He still can't meet my gaze.

"You two dated for about a month when you were diagnosed with stage two brain cancer. Meningioma tumors. You were handling it just fine, to be honest.

You started treatment immediately and were scheduled for surgery. But it ate away at Cragen. He asked his parents for help. They were developing some sort of experimental drug to minimize your tumors and keep the cancer from spreading.

"But instead of talking to you about it, the idiot did the unthinkable. He gave you doses of different crap in secret, dissolving it in your tea or shooting you up in the arm while you were sleeping. You gained some of your strength back, but you were acting funny. Like, you could suddenly see and hear things so much clearer, but your pain tolerance worsened. I remember you tripped down my apartment steps once after one of your treatments, and your acted like you'd broken a leg even though it was nothing but a mild sprain. It was maddening, Kaiya.

"He fed you a variety of drugs for about two weeks before you finally figured it out. He told you he did it because he couldn't live in a world without you. So, you dumped him. And rightfully so," he amends when he sees my miserable pout. "He should have talked to you about it first. But no. He did it for his own selfish reasons." Barris pauses to prod the fire with the stick Emmett used earlier. The flames are considerably lower now, barely licking above the wood. Barris bows his head lower. "You disappeared not long after that. We thought maybe he had something to do with it, but he was gone, too. Nowhere to be found. I have no doubt in my mind now that he took you away for some sort of experimentation."

I swallow the lump in my throat. "Do you think whatever he did to me is causing my nightmares about Dylan?"

He shrugs. "Maybe? I'm not sure. Tell me more about these dreams."

So, I tell Barris about every gruesome end Dylan's met in my nightmares. I share in too much detail the helplessness I feel in the dreams, how I can never save him, how every sound and touch feels too realistic to be nothing more than a night terror. I even tell him briefly about the nightmares Dylan has about me.

"Do you think we are somehow connected by whatever Cragen did to us?"

"It's hard to say," Barris says, "but anything is possible. I do remember you having freaky dreams before all this, though. Something strange would happen and you'd say 'Barris, I had a dream about this!' I never believed it until you told me one of the jocks in the high school gym was going to smash a fifty-pound weight on his knee. *That* was freaky."

"So, I'm just a freak. Great."

"I always knew you were a freak," he flashes a wicked grin, finally able to look at me.

But I can't return his smile.

"So, if the dreams weren't Cragen's doing, what about this mark?"

"What mark?"

I turn my back to Barris and move my hair to reveal my bare neck. I explain what I can about it. Barris hums skeptically.

"I don't know what this is," he says, honesty ringing with every word. "But it does remind me of something…"

"What?" I plea.

"Have you ever looked at an infected up close?"

"No. I'm usually concentrating on getting away from them."

"Just take a good look at their skin next time," he says.

I simply nod.

"Any other questions you wanna get off your chest before you go to sleep?" Barris asks as I return to my spot.

"Just one. Have you ever been to Cragen's compound?"

Barris stares at me, hesitant to answer.

"Yes," he admits with a sigh. He runs a hand over his greasy buzzcut. "I've been there. And maybe one day I'll go back. If he's still 'practicing' there, maybe we can save anyone else he has captive. Though truthfully, I'd rather not go back to that place."

"Why? What happened?"

"That's more than one question," he snaps.

I wait. The fire is gone. Only glowing embers remain.

"I found his compound a few months after you disappeared." Barris' voice shakes. From anger? Regret? Fear? "I found it untouched on the outskirts, so I snuck in to look for you. But I found something awful. I can't describe to you what they were doing in detail, but I can tell you that Cragen, his parents, and some other random doctors were torturing people and injecting them with some sort of serum."

He pauses as if to let me ask a question. When I don't, he continues, his hands quivering with his tone.

"I'd never harmed someone before this. You have to know that. I'm sure you know how I feel about killing. But if I hadn't done it, those people would

143

have died. I got four people out that night and barely escaped myself."

"What did you do?" the question rings acidic and strong.

"I killed Cragen's parents."

Chapter 13

I'm right about the nightmare. As per usual.

It's not about the hotel, though.

I've returned to the dim lit room where Cragen and Scott terrorized us previously. I'm pinned to the same cold gurney, my body rendered immobile. The only difference is I can move my head to look around the room.

Cracked cement walls encase this terrifying surgical room. There are glass cases of medicine bottles and tonic veils on either side of me, the various colorful liquids glistening under the surgical light heads. The lightbulbs are slightly yellow with age. I crane my head to see the area behind me, but all I can see are two more operating tables, one stained crimson along the arm straps.

I snap my head back when I hear the door slam shut. The four doctors I recognize from previous encounters appear. They all wear their familiar white robes, but the dark-haired doctor has blood splattered down his front.

I do my best to remain perfectly still as they circle me.

"I don't think we should do this," the red-headed doctor says, placing his hands on the table for support. I feel the heat radiating from his skin just inches from my arms.

"Why is that doctor?" The dark-haired doctor asks, preparing a syringe. This doctor seems familiar. Something about his hollow cheeks and dimpled chin.

"It didn't work with the last two patients. What makes you think it will work on her?" The red head demands.

"It's obvious, isn't it? She's special."

"He's right," the blonde doctor defends. *Cragen.*

"She's recovering splendidly. Besides, she's survived so many injections. I'm confident she can survive this one."

"But this is different. *If* she does survive, she won't remember anything. We can't take her memories of her human life." The red-headed doctor says, blue-eyes ablaze and arms crossed tightly over his chest. "This isn't right."

"We can't let her live knowing we did this to her," says Cragen. "This was the agreement. Now that she survived the tests and is in recovery, we have to take her memories from her before we can terminate the cancerous cells."

"And risk killing her in the process? Do we really want to risk killing the only successful experiment we have?"

Cragen cringes at the word *killing*, looking down at my still body before turning to the dark-haired doctor.

Of course! That's why he looks familiar! That's Cragen's father!

"It's a risk we are willing to take," Cragen's father speaks up. Though Cragen opens his mouth to object, he remains inaudible. Meanwhile, his father fills a syringe with a black liquid. Something cold and wet brushes against my arm. Without moving my head, I look down to see the quiet blonde-haired woman sterilizing the crease in my elbow with a cotton ball and alcohol. Perhaps this is Cragen's mother?

"Well, I'm not," the red-haired doctor says, then he stomps towards the door.

"Nolan, please," Cragen tries to stop him.

Nolan. The sound of his name sends a violent shiver down my body. I know this name. I've heard it before.

"Please, don't," I say in a raspy voice, barely audible. Four pairs of eyes spin in my direction. Each of the doctors step forward to stare at me. The red-haired doctor, Nolan, stands the furthest from me, his eyes wide and nervous.

"What did you say?" The red-headed doctor begs as they all gather around the table.

I clear my throat. "Please. P-please. Don't." Speaking hurts my chest, burns my throat. It's like I haven't spoken in weeks!

146

"You see? We have to do it." Cragen's father brings the needle down to my arm.

"NO! Please!" I try to yank my arm away, but it won't obey me. The needle breaks my skin, and the warm liquid spreads up in my veins like wildfire. Then everything slowly goes numb, and my eyes begin to droop.

"It's for the best," he says to his son as they all leave the room. I drift further and deeper, eyelids heavy.

But before I give into the drowsiness, Dylan's voice pulls me back. He's suddenly bent over me, unfastening my restraints.

How did he get in here?

"Kaiya, can you hear me?" he asks as he shakes me lightly. He scans over my body for damage. His eyes rest on the needle prick in my arm. "Oh, what did they do to you?"

But before he can pull me off the gurney, someone slits his throat with a scalpel. The room goes black before I can see who.

****

I awake on the floor of my tent, the ground underneath cold on my back even through my t-shirt. I rolled around so much in my sleep that my sleeping bag has formed a knot around my ankles. My hair is plastered to my neck, sweat pooling under my breasts and down the center of my back. I free my feet and unzip the tent.

It's much too early to be awake. Though the sky has lightened some overhead, the sun is nowhere in sight. It is light enough that I can see to rebuild our fire

147

for a quick breakfast before we set out for the compound.

The morning breeze cools my feverish body, making some traces of the nightmare vanish. One thing sticks in my head though as I collected more cambium shavings for a fire.

Nolan.

Who is Nolan?

What was he doing in my dream?

Why didn't he stop Cragen and his parents?

What did he do to me*?*

More importantly, *was it real*?

No, surely not, or Dylan wouldn't have been there. I don't think I knew Dylan pre-apocalypse.

I can't shake the feeling that these bizarre dreams have some truth to them. They are difficult to interpret, though. Why am I dreaming of this Nolan guy, and why did he let them take my memory away? What does it all mean?

Clearly there are some secrets. And I'm bound determined to figure it out.

The tree I collect shavings from is small, but the closest one to our campsite in the meadow. It's not until I finish and glance up the tree towards the lightening sky that I notice it.

Etchings. In several trees, all in a line leading deeper into the dark, in the opposite direction as Cragen's compound.

Kaiya 33. Kaiya 33.

KAIYA.

"I don't think there's a need to rush out."

We're gathered around the fire again. We just finished scrounging for something to eat –

squirrels…yum! – and took a few minutes to genuinely enjoy this fine morning. Death's stench can't seem to touch me here. I feel nothing. This is the most I've smiled in the last few days. My injuries are nearly invisible now. Dylan's walking much better today. Barris' presence adds an essence of nostalgia to my particularly good mood. For the first time in what feels like an eternity, I'm carefree.

Until I look over towards my name in the trees. Then a whole new mess of worries barrel toward me.

Where does it lead? Who left it there? And why would this mysterious artist want to lead us in the opposite direction of our intended destination?

It couldn't have been Cragen or the mongrils. They wouldn't have hesitated to capture us. They wouldn't wait quietly amongst the branches for us to follow the new trail.

I have no other suspects. I don't know any other living beings – if there are any others alive, that is.

So, who did this? How do they know me? What do they want from me?

"Why do you say that?" I ask Dylan, forcing myself back to the moment.

"I ran the perimeter early on my watch," he states. His eyes are warmer today, more golden. Mesmerizing, yet destructive. Uncertainty twists my stomach. Dylan clears his throat, gaze focused on me. "No tracks. No signs of anything living for nearly a mile. I think we can take a minute to collect ourselves before we continue on."

If Dylan didn't notice anything out of the ordinary on his perimeter check, then my name must have been etched in after his shift, which also means no one else has found the etchings yet.

I barely nod. "Just for a few minutes. The mongrils could be anywhere."

"How about a little cardio before we go?" Scott suggests, stretching his oversized arms as he stands.

Jacklyn's eyes flash. She jumps up. "Count me in!"

Rylie, Kade and I volunteer to pack up camp while the others take turns 'training.' Jacklyn takes Scott down. Scott catches Dylan off guard and takes him down, enjoying it a little too much. Barris takes Emmett down. Emmett and Dylan tie.

"You should go show my brother how it's done," Rylie chuckles as we watch Dylan and Emmett struggle.

I laugh out loud. "I don't think he's ready to handle me."

"So, you can take down big guy over there?"

"I'm not sure which one is 'big guy,' but yes."

"Oh, I'd pay my hidden bottle of whiskey to see that!" Rylie says.

Kade shoots him a bewildered look. "You have whiskey on you?"

"Not with me," Rylie corrects. "It's hidden under my mattress at the community. Do you like whiskey?"

Kade shrugs innocently. "Never tried it. That's how Barris and I met, you know. He found me in an old grocery store wandering down the liquor aisle. Thought I was an infected." Kade rolls his sleeve to reveal a round scar on his upper arm. "He was a terrible shot back then. I just wanted to try some, since there's no age restriction now."

"Wait, how old are you?"

Kade's grin turns sheepish. "About 19."

19?! Kade was just a teenaged boy when the world went to hell! So young. So innocent. And he never got to experience the finer things in life. But, for that matter, have *I* had the chance to experience those things, either? Perhaps if my memory hadn't been stripped from me…Dylan groans

I shake my head. "Rylie, how's about a wager?"

"Oh?" he says, arms cross.

"You pick my opponent. I win, Kade gets that bottle of whiskey and I get to keep that picture you have of me."

"You mean the one of you and Cragen you have hidden in your pocket?" he accuses.

"How did you…?"

"I'm not stupid," he snaps, then quickly backtracks. "Okay. You win, you keep the picture and Kade gets my whiskey. And if you lose, you tell my brother everything you said about him last night."

It appears I may have underestimated Rylie a bit.

"Okay, deal."

But before we can shake on it, Scott is walking past us toward the trees.

"What is that?" he wonders aloud as he progresses to a jog. I follow behind in horror as he goes to the carved-up trees I've been avoiding all morning.

Only now there's a ring of arrows protruding just above the markings.

Someone was here – or may still be here – and we didn't even hear them. How did we not hear them? No, how did *I* not hear them?

To my dismay, the entire group rushes to circle the tree. I keep my distance.

151

"Where do you think it leads?" Scott asks.

"Nowhere good," Barris says, tracing the K with his forefinger.

I clear my throat quietly. "We should get moving," I say, but I can't keep the nerves from scraping out.

Dylan scrunches an accusatory frown at me. "You *knew* this was here?"

"Why didn't you tell us, Kaiya?" Jacklyn demands.

"It'll only take us off course." I avoid the harsh glares.

"Do you think it's the same person who carved your name in that arm?"

I train my gaze on the carving in the tree. The lettering looks similar to the etches in that severed arm at the gas station, aside from two subtle differences.

"No. The 'K' and 'Y' look different. It's someone else."

"If someone knows we are here, we need to move," Scott interjects, grazing roughly into my shoulder as he passes. Everyone follows him except Dylan and Barris.

Barris yanks an arrow from the tree.

"Kaiya, I don't think this was Cragen's doing."

"But who, then?" Dylan asks, his voice a whispered hiss. "Mongrils?"

Barris shakes his head. "No. Their arrows are simplistic. *These* are painted black.

"But why take the time to paint them? Unless they're not homemade."

I remain silent as they speculate. If this wasn't done by the mongrils, then who? *Who* would want to get my attention like this?

Barris saunters off to join the others in fetching our gear. Dylan moves to stand in front of me, arms crossed.

"You knew this was here." It's no longer a question.

I nod. "I saw it this morning. I'd hoped no one would notice…"

"Why didn't you tell someone?" Dylan groans. "This person could be out there watching us right now, just waiting for the chance to get to you."

"No. Whoever this is, they wouldn't do that."

"What makes you so sure?" he snaps, then motions for me to follow him.

"Just a hunch."

Chapter 14

"We're getting close," Rylie announces beside his brother.

We're in an overgrown field now, traveling alongside the dirt road on the outskirts of the neighboring county. Two crumbling farmhouses are the only visible structures for miles.

"How can you tell?" Kade asks, skipping behind Barris. How can this young thing be so cheery? So full of energy?

"The compound lies just past the tree line a couple miles ahead," Rylie explains plainly.

The tension, a thick white aura with blasting rays of violet poking through its mists, covers the group like a concentrated blizzard. It's all come down to this. I'm going to finally get the answers I've sought, the closure I crave, the realizations I need, maybe even the memories I've lost. So why am I suddenly overwhelmed with failing scenarios, all which end with the same three people meeting a terrible end?

Can't escape it in my dreams, and now I can't escape it here.

"Maybe we should stop and come up with a plan," Barris suggests.

I glare at him. Though I don't want to confront whatever lies ahead of us, why delay the inevitable?

"We're sneaking in," I say, more baritone in my voice than intended. "*That's* the plan."

"I think we need more of a plan than that, Kaiya," Jacklyn says. Her voice is warm, but trembles ever so slightly at the end.

"Do we know how many mongrils might be there?" Scott asks, arms cross. "Maybe if we know, we can weigh our odds of getting in and creeping around."

"Not a clue," Barris says. "Last I knew, there were only a handful of them."

"Definitely more than that now," Rylie mutters.

"How many entrances are there?" I ask.

"Only one that I know of," Barris glances around the group.

"I snuck Dylan back out through a window," Rylie states. "Could be a way in."

At the mention of his name, I chance a look at Dylan. His face has paled, eyes narrowed on me with...fear? Concern? Indecision? His brown stare begs me to reconsider this mess. To think about our nightmares. Does he think one of the prophecies will be fulfilled if we enter the compound? Is the ice in this look about his life on the line or mine? I can practically see the wheels in his head turning.

"Dylan?"

His name escapes my lips. He looks down with shame.

"I'm not walking into Cragen's lair without a plan," Dylan states bluntly.

"That's fine," I say, frustration warming my cheeks. "Y'all want to be scared little girls, I'll go in alone."

"The hell you will," Barris snaps at the same time as Dylan and Scott.

"We just need to think this through first," Jacklyn lays a hand on me.

Scott bobs his head towards one of the farmhouses. "How about we stop for a bit, rest, come up with a plan?"

"Sure, sure," I wave him forward.

The grass slaps my knees, somehow adding to my anger. The house isn't far, yet the walk makes me grind my teeth.

They knew this is what we came here to do. They knew the plan – or lack thereof. Why can't we just get it over with?

Yes, I'm being unreasonable. I'm overreacting. I'm aware. But I can't talk myself down in my mind. The only thing I can think about in this moment is getting inside that compound.

Until I trip over something and faceplant.

I groan, twisting round to see what tripped me up, and freeze.

It's just an infected. A dead infected woman with a bashed in skull. She has dirty hair the same length and color as mine, but in a perfectly curly mess. Her bloodshot eyes remain wide open despite the fact her heart doesn't beat, and she's wearing a blue tank with daisy-duke booty shorts. But these aren't the first things I notice.

No. The first thing I notice is her *skin*.

She's ghostly white, as most the infected are after years of undead aging, her veins sticking out harshly on her arms, legs, especially her neck and face. They're dark purple, black in most spots, branching out in sharp angles. Pretty sure veins and arteries aren't supposed to look like this. It's sickening. Not because it looks painful and deadly – oh and does it! – but because it reminds me of my talk with Barris.

"Just take a good look at their skin next time," he had said. My mark reminded him of this. My blemished skin reminded him of these harshly visible arteries permanently burned with infection.

"Kaiya!" Scott and Dylan help me up. Scott holds my arm to steady me.

"You okay?" Dylan asks, brows furrowed.

But I can't look away from her. Her veins, thick and darkened by the radiation that made her an infected, that ripped her life away from her. Do I –?

"Fine," I say tersely. "Just fine."

****

Most everyone is sleeping in the living area, aside from Scott and Dylan, who play rock-paper-scissors for god-knows-what. Jacklyn and I sneak away to what used to be the kitchen, but the ceiling has fell in, covering the appliances in rotted wood and insulation. I tell her about part of my conversation with Barris and about my sudden revelation when I tripped over that infected woman in the field. I start spilling out theories to her, most of which don't make a lick of sense. After I wave my bite mark on my wrist under her nose, she's had enough.

157

"There's no point speculating about this, Kaiya," she interrupts. "You're going to drive yourself bat-shit-crazy reading this much into it. Besides, you'll have your answers soon anyway."

I nod reluctantly. "You're right. Sorry. I'm just wound a little tight is all."

And then Jacklyn hugs me. This is a big deal for her, seeing how she rejects all displays of affection. Seems kind of odd to me, especially since there isn't hardly anyone left in the world to judge her PDA, but that's just how she is. The first time she kissed Emmett in front

of Scott and I, she was so embarrassed. But it was a spur of the moment thing. He almost died! Of course, she was going to kiss him. Boy, did she get a lot of crap about it later.

So, for her to be hugging me now is unbelievable. I squeeze her back. When she pulls away, her eyes are filled with warmth and peace.

"Don't worry so much. Cragen won't even know what hit him."

She pretends not to notice my cringe and joins the others.

I retire to the living area after a few moments alone. Jacklyn's fast asleep now, snuggled under Emmett's arm. Even Scott is snoring softly. Just Dylan and I left.

"You know I wouldn't let you go alone, right?" he says after a minute.

"I hope so," is all I can mumble.

"You better know so." Dylan's eyes ablaze, he moves over to sit beside me. "I wouldn't come all this way just to let you run into fire."

I say nothing, averting my gaze to the floor. My friends wouldn't let me run into fire. Scott, Jacklyn, Emmett...Barris is family, so he wouldn't let me dive headfirst into an empty pool, either...but why does Dylan care? If something did happen to me, wouldn't his nightmares stop? Shouldn't he hope for that?

He's silent, too, as he twines his fingers with mine. His thumb traces the back of my hand, sending a new warmth with the ever-present shock of his touch.

"You know," I whisper, barely loud enough for his ears, "you don't have to worry about me."

Dylan's teeth gnash audibly. "It's not exactly something I can just turn off."

"What I mean is, it won't be your fault when it happens. You don't have to do anything to stop it."

"You're only saying that because you don't want the opposite to happen."

"You're right. I don't want you in the way." I think about him jumping between me and the mongrils, about the knife plunged into him as I fall into a dark abyss, and cringe.

"Why?" he asks.

"Isn't it obvious?" Because I'm stupid. Because I care about you. Because I want to know you better. Because I don't know what's going to happen, but whatever it is, I'd rather it happen to me. Because I won't be able to live with myself otherwise.

"Maybe not as obvious as you think."

Maybe not.

"Can I ask you something?"

"Ask away."

"You said you were trapped in Cragen's compound, and Rylie got you out."

"Yes…?"

"What did they do to you?"

Dylan sighs. "I won't go into much detail. I was there for a few days, I think. They withdrew some blood and left to run some tests. They must have been disappointed that I didn't have morus in me. When they came back, they injected me with something. The mongrils tormented me for a while before Rylie found me." Dylan hikes up his shirt to reveal a long silvery slit along his navel. "I've still got the scars as a reminder."

Our hands remain intertwined. I offer his sweaty palm a squeeze.

"Is that why you're scared to go back?"

"Scared?" Dylan releases my hand. "I'm terrified."

That settles it, a voice in my head declares.

Dylan distracts himself by twirling a strand of my hair. Blush thickens. He then brushes my hair back, revealing the mark.

"Do you mind?" he asks.

Suddenly aware of his proximity, I gulp and nod.

Dylan sweeps my hair over the opposite shoulder to completely reveal the stretch of black up my neck. A single fingertip traces the mark up to the back of my scalp, then down again to trace the perpendicular lines. An involuntary shiver ripples through me.

"Looks like ticks on a timeline," he says quietly, pulling away.

Ticks on a timeline? Almost like they mark the most eventful moments permanently on my body?

Come to think of it, I notice what I call the 'growing' pain on my mark after something big happens, like a near death experience. I remember the

160

pain snaking up my back when I saw my name on that severed arm in the gas station bathroom, and again when Blair hung Yuna's brother from a tree, and when Blair and I had our knock-down drag-out, and when Dylan broke his ankle, and when I escaped the hotel...

What in the hell is going on with this mark?

I must be making a funny face because Dylan watches me now.

"Does it hurt?" he asks.

I shake my head and clear my facial expressions. "Not right now."

Dylan leans his head against the wall, eyes closed, and sighs.

"Why did you come out here?" I blurt and abruptly cover my mouth. Luckily, no one stirs. Then, more quietly: "And don't say to keep the nightmares from coming true. I know that's part of it, but there's got to be more."

"I came to make sure you don't get hurt."

"Aaaand...?"

"Aaaand," he says, eyes still closed, "I continued to follow along as an excuse to get to know you." He pauses, opening his eyes to peak at me under his lashes. "Is that what you wanted to hear?"

"Maybe?" I laugh. "I'm not sure what I wanted to hear, honestly."

"Now answer me this," he angles himself to face me. "Why were you so willing to go with the mongrils when they came looking for you?"

I frown at him. "You were being held captive. Rylie was passed out. They would have ripped through the community just to find me, for god-knows what reason. Was there really another option?"

"There's always another option," Dylan's voice sounds thick and solemn. I yawn loudly, spurring a crooked smile from him.

"What?"

"What do you say we forget everything for a few minutes? Forget Cragen, the compound, our nightmares. Forget that the world's nearly desolate and overran with infected. Forget that Scott and Jacklyn will lecture you about it later," he snickers, mainly to himself. "I'm sure Rylie will lecture me, too."

I blink. "What are you talking about?"

Dylan's crooked smile widens. He pats on the floor directly beside him, then offers an open arm to me. "Come here."

I can't suppress my grin. "Tempting. But I should take watch."

"*I* will take first watch. You're obviously tired. Close your eyes for a few minutes. I'll keep a lookout from right beside you."

After I surrender, his well-sculpted arm wraps around me. The static makes me jump, but warmth soon replaces the strange shock. My shoulders slump as the rest of my body gives in to exhaustion. Dylan releases a comfortable sigh.

"I could get used to this," he mutters, his voice huskier than normal.

But he can't get used to it. He *shouldn't* get used to it.

****

"What?! What do you want from me?!"

I'm stuck once again in my dreams. Barris is dead by me or the mongrils. I'm not sure, and I've cried over his dead body for what felt like an eternity.

But then Barris opens his eyes. He stares up at me with an accusing scowl. He stands, despite his broken limbs. I tumble backwards to get away from him. He hobbles towards me. *What is he going to do?*

I back right into Scott. He smiles at me. A sweet, gentle smile. A smile that in no way matches the atmosphere of this nightmare! Then he takes a step towards me, offering his hand…only there is no hand. Only a bloody stump of an arm.

I retreat from them both when I bump into Jacklyn. Her blood is warm on the back of my arm where we collide. She frowns, her eyes filled with red tears.

Forget this! I sprint away.

And run into a big mess of people.

Emmett. Kade. Rylie. Even Yuna.

They're all covered in blood. They're all dead.

They close in on me, muttering something I don't understand. Their faces start to swirl together. I'm losing my mind!

I beg time and time again. "What?! What do you want from me?!" But I can't get a straight answer through the synchronized garbling of words. I curl up on the ground in the fetal position with my hands over my ears.

Suddenly, the mindless murmurs stop. And a pair of warm, gentle hands touch my face. I open my eyes slowly, and immediately wish I hadn't.

It's Dylan. The one person missing from this nightmare.

He is dead, too.

His throat has been slashed with a jagged blade. Blood pours down the open wound and covers the front of his shirt. His perfect face is bruised, with purpling marks covering his cheeks and his left eye. He has a fat, cut lip and a distorted nose.

The others still stand in a circle around us, but they're no longer circling. Everyone smiles now. What the hell do they have to be so happy about? They're dead!

Dylan holds a hand out to me. I take it reluctantly, sobbing and shaking with fear.

"Did I do this?" I ask him between awkward choking noises.

No answer.

"Are you dead because of me?"

He still doesn't answer. He just smiles at me. The same smile I love to see, despite the fat lip.

"I'm so sorry, I didn't mean to…" But I don't know that. Maybe I did mean to. I mean, I don't know *exactly* how he died. Maybe I snapped. Or maybe Cragen killed him trying to get to me. Or maybe it was a terrible accident I caused. Or maybe he came after me and I had to defend myself.

Dylan opens his mouth to speak, then closes it again. He looks around at the others. Still smiling. *Why are they smiling?!*

I blink. They're gone. And I'm all alone

Then I hear a new laugh. *His* laugh. How am I able to recognize his laugh when I can't even remember him?

I twist to find his face inches from mine.

Cragen smiles, a smile so sickening and wide it raises the hairs on my arms. I'm frozen as he walks around me, stopping only to ruffle my hair. I shiver. Cragen steps back three feet, dramatically raises his right hand, and snaps his fingers.

With a thud, bodies hit the floor. Scott, Jacklyn, everyone. Dylan lies crumpled and broken at my feet once again, the brown drained from his lifeless eyes.

****

I wake in a cold sweat, as I have many times before. But this feels different. Worse. Much worse. I must not have made any noise, because everyone is asleep, even Dylan. Wasn't he supposed to be the lookout?

After successfully wiggling myself free of his arm, I sit there for a moment and watch him breathe. No doubt he's dreaming about me, too, because his nose scrunches every few seconds while his eyes roll rapidly under the lids. I wonder briefly how gruesome my death is this time. But then the wrinkles on his forehead smooth out, as if the worst of the dream has already passed. He doesn't stir or wake like I do after a nightmare. What's happening now, inside his head?

No matter how hard I try to concentrate on him, the images from my dream won't disappear. They're burned into me, charring what small amount of sanity I have left. A new weight has been added to my shoulders, as Dylan's life isn't the only one dangling over the Reaper's scythe. I'm only one person – a small, insignificant person at that. How am I supposed to protect everyone? What will Cragen have in store for us? How am I supposed to prepare for the worst when I don't even know what to expect?

Or, maybe, I don't have to.

Not sure if it's the drafty house, the darkening sky against the setting sun, or the fact that I'm about to leave my friends that sends violent tremors down my spine. I search through our bags as quietly as possible until I find a jacket to tug over my arms. This is the only thing I bring with me besides my sheathed dagger. No point in bringing supplies. They'll need it more than I will. Creaky boards signal my exit, but thankfully do not disturb the others. I secure the front door before heading out. This should buy them some time for much-needed rest.

The frigid wind whistles through the trees, swaying loose strands of my hair. I pull on my hood and venture into the grass. I only make it a couple yards when I hear a crunch behind me.

"Going somewhere?"

"You're supposed to be asleep."

Barris jumps to block my path, his giant arms crossed tightly in front of him.

"It's my watch. I just finished a perimeter check," he states. "Good thing, too, or I wouldn't have caught you sneaking out."

"Well, get back to it," I shoo him away.

"I have places to go. People to see."

"You mean person?"

I glare at my cousin. "What do you want, Barris?"

"Let me come with you."

NO. Absolutely not. That defeats the whole purpose of me sneaking out and going alone. Of course, I don't say any of this out loud. I can't find my voice for some reason.

Barris continues to look down on me, his dark eyes pleading. If I tell him no, what's to stop him from waking the others? He'll tell them I took off, that I left them, and they'll try to come after me. But not before he tries – and undoubtably fails – to stop me himself. I don't want to fight my cousin, but I will if I have to.

"Guess I don't have a choice," I hang my head with a sigh. "Let's get out of here before the others get up."

I stride around him. Barris jogs a little to catch up.

"So, what's the plan?"

I shrug. "Wing it."

"Not much of a plan."

"If it gets me there, it'll do just fine."

Chapter 15

"That's it?"

"Yup."

Barris and I squat in the bushes at the base of the hill just outside what looks like a well-aged steel barn, minus the typically large, red barn doors. Instead, there is a short, thick metal entrance with two sets of deadbolts. I see no visible windows, but Rylie had said he escaped through a broken one on the backside of the building.

We sit there for a few minutes, waiting for any signs of movement. But nothing. Nada. Not a single guard or mongril in sight. No infected, either. We didn't even see any on our short journey here.

We creep around back, crouching in the tall grass as much as possible. Sure enough, there is a broken window low enough for us to get in. Still no sign of Cragen's mongrils.

"Maybe the place is empty," Barris says, though there's no optimism in his gruff voice.

But, sure enough, someone had been here. The one tree close enough to the building bares an arrow in its trunk, just like the arrows planted on the *Kaiya 33* path. Whoever this is, they knew I didn't go the way they wanted. Maybe the mystery guest has already come and gone. Or maybe they're waiting for us?

I do another quick scan of the area and rush to the window.

Barris must've spotted the black arrows, too.

"Kaiya," he hisses. "Get *back* here."

Do I listen? *Ha*!

I peak inside. Not a soul in sight. I crawl through the window, slicing my palm on a shard protruding from the frame. I grind my teeth and dart to the shadows. It's not deep.

"Dammit, Kaiya," Barris curses as he takes his sweet time tumbling through the window. Even in an undead world, Barris remains a 'poky-puppy.'

"Shh! Could you be any louder?"

"Sorry."

I squint and strain my eyes, but I can't see anything past the allotted light from the window. It'll be dark out in another hour.

Barris digs around in one of his many pockets. He pulls out a miniature flashlight and a pocketknife. He hands me the light. I snicker at him.

"What?" he asks.

"Nothing, nothing," I dismiss with a grin. I seem to remember Barris collecting flashlights as a kid. And he always wore ugly pants with lots of pocket space. On the one hand, this is practical. He's come prepared. On the other hand, though, it's simply nostalgic. At least *he* didn't lose his personality after the apocalypse.

I click on the flashlight.

Cragen's compound is exactly as I imagined it would be. Several gurneys line the main floor, all accompanied by trays with surgical tools. There are no privacy curtains to separate them like there would be in a medical wing. A glass case lines the wall closest to us, but the doors have been shattered. I move between the gurneys, Barris close beside me. Each sheet is stained red and brown. Even the cement floor has splotchy stains. I try not to think about how the marks got there as we walk to the loft stairs.

It's a remarkably small loft. Looks more like an office. Binders and notebooks litter the desk and the bookshelf, each marked with a number. Above the bookshelf is a framed picture. I stare at it for a moment.

It's the same as the picture in my pocket.

But why would Cragen keep a picture of the two of us together after everything he has done?

Without much thought, I smash the glass frame with my fist. Barris jumps back a little, notices the picture, and shrugs. *At least someone gets it.* Of course, Barris of all people could empathize with my distain for the man I hardly remember. He continues to scan the room as if nothing happened.

"What a dump," Barris whispers under his breath. I nod in agreeance, then sift through the numbered binders. I pause on a notebook labeled *PROJECT MORUS*. Could this be about the morus cells Dylan mentioned?

Barris bumps me with his elbow, then points to the floor. I follow his finger to a fallen binder. On the spine is the number 33. It lays just in front of a small closet. There's a nervous *thud, thud, thud* coming from it.

Before Barris can argue, I equip my dagger and hand him the flashlight, then motion for him to keep it aimed on the door. I step forward, turning the knob slowly, and thrust it open.

"AH!" a man squeals, jumping back as far as the closet will allow. He cowers at the knife pointed at him, covering his untidy red locks with trembling hands. But he locks eyes with me, and his hands instantly stop shaking. He straightens slowly, despite my still-poised knife.

"Kaiya. It's about time." The familiarity of his voice makes me flinch.

"Who are you?" I demand.

"I warned you not to come this way," he says. "Why did you come this way?"

"That was *you*?" My dagger moves forward an inch.

"Who are you?" Barris repeats my question. He then pulls the man out by his collar. This guy looks like he may wet his pants.

"Whoa, Whoa," he exclaims, hands held in defense. "I'm Davic, Davic Nolan."

Nolan.

Nolan from my nightmares?

"You said you warned me." I lower my blade ever so slightly. "Are you the one who carved my name into all those trees?"

"I had to do something." Nolan rolls his eyes. "But you didn't follow the trail, as I suspected you wouldn't, so I knew I had to beat you here."

Barris turns Davic Nolan to face him now, eyebrows furrowed, and face flushed. Nolan cringes away from Barris' intense glower.

"Why are you following Kaiya? What do you want with her?"

"I needed to get to her before Cragen did," he explains in a rushed breath, "to explain the past. To warn her. To warn all of you."

"Warn us about what?" I demand.

"It's a long story, but I can explain everything." His voice is calmer, but still cracks slightly under his pseudo composure. "Please. Let's sit and talk. We'll need to clear out of here before Cragen's mongrils discover that you're here."

After a short moment of deliberation, I give Barris the nod. He releases Nolan.

"Thank you," he sighs. He grabs the rolling chair from beside the desk and pops a squat. Barris leans beside the closet, arms crossed. If I didn't know my cousin better, I'd say he's trying too hard to come off as intimidating to this wee little man. I sit cross-legged and reach for the binder I forgot about on the floor.

"Let's keep it simple," I say. "First, I want you to tell me about morus."

"How much do you know about morus cells?"

I shrug. "Just that Cragen's interested in them."

"Oh, he's more than interested in them," Nolan scoffs. "I was working under Cragen's parents, Cym and Magna, when an army lieutenant approached us about the morus project. The United States government inserted itself into the fourth World War between Asia, Europe, and South Africa. They wrongfully decided

172

chemical warfare was the best way to end it. They were gonna fight nukes with more nukes.

"But someone must've given away our plans. Word got out, as did the formula used for the morus project, and we were beat to the punch. Bombs dropped in California. Hundreds of people were killed on impact, while even more were infected by the radioactive gas, a toxic plague *I* helped create, no less!" Disgust colors his cheeks as he clears his throat and continues, eyeing the floor. "More bombs dropped over Washington, Colorado, South Dakota, even smaller nukes here in Missouri. The infected people became very sick, their brains swelling from the toxicity, leaving them mad and ravenous.

"The infected spread the radiation to others through their teeth and nails, and there was no cure for the infection once it set in. So, the lieutenant came to us again, this time asking us to create a vaccination, in hopes that no one else would contract it should they come into contact with an infected. I thought it impossible. Vaccines are for viruses, *not* radiation. But Cym failed to tell anyone that the project indeed contained a newly discovered pathogen called the moruris virus."

Barris grunts, peering through his lashes at Nolan in frustration. "I don't know much about viruses. Think you could dumb it down a bit for us here on out, Doc?"

Nolan sighs. "Alright. Without going into too much scientific detail, a vaccine was impossible. But Cym was able to create a cell from the rapidly mutating moruris virus. He believed the morus cells could not only protect the body from infection, but also repair

173

and strengthen the body. The infection spread so fast that we had to skip safety testing on lab rats and go straight to human testing. The first fifteen or so trials were failures. The cells acted less as antibodies and more as parasites, draining the life out of their hosts.

"With the world turning to shit and infection spreading, the government would no longer fund the trials. They moved on to find someone else to make the 'vaccine'. But Cym and Magna were obsessed with perfecting the morus cells, specifically so they could protect Cragen and themselves from infection. If they were going to continue to experiment on people, they'd have to do so in secret. And that's exactly what they did. I didn't realize they were kidnapping young people and administering the cells until *you* were the thirty-third patient on the gurney," he gestures at me sadly.

"Me?" I lean into the conversation.

"Yes. I entered the lab that day to find Cragen in a heated argument with his parents. Cym and Magna stood over you with IV tubes and syringes. I could tell by the thick tension in the room that you were not meant to be there."

"Did Cragen bring me in?" my throat tightens around my words like a noose. I cough to loosen the snare. "What did he do to me?"

"I don't know," Nolan answers honestly. "Cragen was definitely upset about you being there, so I don't think he had a hand in it. But it doesn't matter. He's just as guilty. He helped Cym and Magna experiment on you for days."

"So, the cells worked on me? Why? How?"

"I'm not entirely sure, but I know you were extremely weak when they gave you the morus. Before you, we had only tried the cells on healthy subjects. You were our first dying patient. Maybe the cells had enough to repair that they didn't overwhelm and consume your body." He watches my expression warily, then quickly adds, "That's all speculation, of course."

"So, what exactly did you guys do to her?" Barris growls. I shoot him a warning to 'cool it.'

"Well, the experimentation process was brutal," Nolan says slowly. "They let the cells repair you, then they'd inject you with a disease or a virus and observe as your body fought off the illness. Each time you overcame it, they'd give you another and record your progress. But it drove Cragen mad to think you may be fighting for your life, so he did the unthinkable."

"Which is?"

"He put himself in your shoes. He injected himself with malaria, then gave himself the morus cells."

"What good did that do?" Barris scoffs.

"None what-so-freaking ever. He just didn't want Kaiya to do it alone. It was almost sweet, in a twisted sort of way, until Magna wanted to test the dermal and muscular repair."

That doesn't sound good. "The what?" I ask.

"Please don't make me explain," Nolan begs.

We wait silently.

Nolan growls, as if the subject matter is pure cruelty. "They tortured you. They'd take a scalpel and place hundreds of cuts on your body, each deeper than the last, and watch as you healed. Then they'd do it all over again."

I cringe.

"Naturally, Magna wouldn't let Cragen participate in *that* trial. I'm ashamed that I stuck by them as long as I did. It wasn't until they decided to give you a dangerous memory-revoking injection that I finally checked out."

Memory-revoking injection. Just like in my nightmare…

"That's why I don't remember anything?"

Nolan nods. "After your recovery, they 'deluded' your concentrated strand of morus cells and gave it to a few others as a vaccine. But after they moved you all to a new location, Cym and Magna finally got what they had coming to them. Someone broke into their lab, slaughtered them, and destroyed all their vials of morus."

Barris shifts awkwardly. Even though what he did to Cym and Magna was mostly deserved, his guilty grimace confesses only to the floor. Nolan doesn't notice, or at least he doesn't show any sign of it. But I can't help but wonder what went through Barris' mind when he dropped them.

"Then what happened?" Barris asks, tripping over his words.

"Well, it's kind of embarrassing," Nolan starts, looking up at me through his lashes as if to plead for forgiveness. "I knew where they took you and those others – two big guys, a scrawny red-head, and a little blonde girl – so I decided to break you out before Cragen would come back for you all. But when I got there, infected were swarming in. I had to take you out to my van one at a time. I got you secured first, then went back for the others…"

Nolan's eyes glass over, like he's being transported back to the exact moment where his guilt originates, like he's stuck in an infinite loop of bad decisions and has to keep watching the events unfold over and over, like he's falling into an abyss with no end, into a nightmare I'm all too familiar with...

"We were cut off from the front door by a herd. I tried to take the blonde girl out the back. There were infected everywhere. No way out except through a small window, and we wouldn't both fit, not in time at least."

Barris fills in the gaps before I can process.

"So, you left her behind."

Nolan nods.

I think back to the day I woke up, no memories, surrounded by people I didn't know – Jacklyn, Emmett, Scott...If Nolan had saved that girl, she would've been there, too. I blink to suppress the image.

"Hang on," I say. "I don't understand what any of this has to do with us now. Why is Cragen looking for me? And why are you so worried about it? If Cragen and I used to be...well, you know...then surely he won't hurt me."

Nolan laughs. A dark, dry laugh, one that make the lump in my throat plunge.

"Morus didn't affect him like it did you."

"What do you mean?"

"I mean that you were dying," his voice is suddenly flat, lips forming a tight line. "You still are. Your cancer cells multiply. The morus kills the cancer cells, but there's always at least one cell left to multiply. That's the only reason the concentrated

177

morus has worked for you and no one else. As long as there is something in your body for the morus cells to attack, you'll thrive.

"But Cragen's different. He injected himself with malaria just to test the cells so you wouldn't have to go through it alone. It worked. But the morus killed every virus in his body. What does it have left to attack now? The cells are attacking his brain. He's gone mad. If he doesn't get something deadly into him, like your rapidly growing cancer cells, he will die. And he will do whatever it takes to get what he needs from you."

"So, I just need to give him what he wants, and then he will leave me alone?"

"It's not that simple. Like I said, he's deranged. His thought process has been compromised. His brain cells are deteriorating rapidly. For whatever reason, he believes everyone has been infected with radiation by now, and the morus will save everyone, and yours is the most heavily concentrated. He thinks he has to experiment with your blood to find a cure."

I wait for Nolan to finish, but he won't look me in the eyes. He opens his mouth and closes it repeatedly, like he's biting back word vomit.

"Just spit it out," Barris barks.

Nolan glares at him as the words spill.

"The experiments and the extraction process to make the weakened 'vaccine' almost killed you last time. I doubt you'd survive it again."

My vision blurs at the edges.

Cragen wants my blood. He wants to use me as some sort of guinea pig.

But is he really going to kill me to get what he wants?

And what if he succeeds? *Then* what?

Will Cragen try to "cure" everyone? The people I love?

Dylan escaped the compound once before. What did Cragen do to him then if he didn't have my morus cells?

"Okay, let's back it up a second," Barris says, his brows knit tightly together. "You said Kaiya was dying, then you said, 'you still are.' What did you mean by that?"

"Exactly what it sounds like. Kaiya is going to die. Soon."

Chapter 16

Dylan's dreams were right all along.

I'm going to die. Soon.

Not sure if it will end by a collapsing tree, a knife in the back, an infected, torture from Cragen, cancer, or the overtake of morus cells in my body, but my life will end before long.

Barris decides to do a perimeter check while I peruse through old binders. Once Barris is out of the building, I turn to Nolan and slam my hand on the table.

"I need you to look at something for me, Doc."

He nods, startled. "O-okay?"

I hike up my shirt to give him a good view of my backside. He sucks in a shaky breath and stands.

"Ohhh lordy."

"It started out as a tiny grey mark on my lower back," I explain, "and now it's expanding to my hair line. What the hell is it?"

Nolan traces my mark with a cold finger. I shudder.

"I've only ever seen this in infected individuals. Never in a living, functional human being."

"Is it from infection, then, or something else? Am I going to become one of those things?"

"It's hard to say," he says, and motions for me to pull my shirt down. "There's no easy answer without running some tests, and we don't have the time, power, or equipment to do so."

I groan. "Then can you just speculate for me please?"

"I mean, I –" Nolan clears his throat. "I guess it could be your body reacting to a variety of toxic and foreign elements inside you. What with the morus cells, possible infection, cancer cells, and whatever the hell Cragen injected into your blood stream before all this shit, I imagine your body would be suffering. But you seem to be reacting well physically. Do you have any symptoms? Weakness? Short of breath? Any pain at all?"

180

"No, no. Only pain in my scar when I'm close to infected. Or sometimes a shooting pain up my spine."

"Interesting," he panders, and abruptly turns from me to skip down the steps.

"Doc," I follow close behind. "Please. I need answers."

"There are no easy answers for something like this," he says, throwing his hands in the air. "No explanations I can offer. This isn't my area of expertise. I have no clue what is going on with you, and I can only make guesses as to what will happen."

"Then give me your best guess."

Nolan stops and twists to look at me.

"Please? So, I can move forward?"

He avoids looking directly at me as he speaks. "It might be your nervous system overloading and preparing to shut down."

"Like a computer?"

"Sort of," he says. "I guess that's what it would feel like, with the morus cells battling everything in your body. But it *looks* like maybe the infection or radiation or cancer or whatever-the-hell-it-is may be attacking your nervous system, which would explain why the mark is centralized at your spine and climbing upward."

"So, what do you think is going to happen, if it continues to…grow?"

Nolan sighs. "I don't care to venture that far into these speculations, Kaiya. But I imagine that the mark will continue to grow and expand across your body until whatever-it-is consumes the entirety of the brain. That could take anywhere from two weeks to five years, but I guess that would depend on how rapidly the mark has progressed in the last couple weeks."

I cringe. "What happens then?"

Nolan doesn't respond.

Barris climbs back through the window and stares gravely at us.

"What is it?"

"Shhh!" Barris holds a beefy finger up, pointing to the window. After complete silence falls, I'm able to hear it.

Footprints. Several footprints on crunchy grass. Close to the building. Closing in on the window.

I grab Nolan's collar and drag him to the window frame. Barris huddles on the left side, we take the right. I hold a shushing hand up to Nolan, to which he nods, then reach for my blade.

The footsteps grow closer, closer, until a shadow looms from the window's limited light. I hold my breath instinctively. Nolan glances at me, eyes wide with nerves.

First a hand braces the windowsill. After falsely determining the coast is clear, a large line-backer man climbs through the window and starts forward. Blade poised, I peal myself from the wall and charge the person while his back was turned. Normally I would try to identify the person before attacking, but my brain is currently absorbed with fear from Nolan's stories. Fear for my friends, fear for my pre-destined short lifespan, fear for facing Cragen at all. My actions seem rational at the time, given the circumstances.

Before I can sink the knife into his shoulder, the intruder grabs my hand and twists until the knife clatters to the floor. He twirls around, my wrist still locked in his fingers, until he's facing me. I hold my elbow high to avoid any damage and use my free hand to grab his throat.

And then I notice that I'm choking –

"Scott? What the hell?" I release him. But he doesn't release me.

"Kaiya? I-I thought…" Scott stutters, still holding my wrist. Cramps work up my captive arm. He puts his chin to the window, then hollers. "It's okay, guys. Coast is clear."

The others file in through the window, Dylan bringing up the rear. They all glare at me. But Dylan's glare remains the sharpest. I can't match his stare, not with Scott still holding my arm in this crushing manner.

I look pointedly between us. "You wanna let me go, or do I have to break your hand?"

"Oh, sorry." Scott releases me.

"You scared the hell out of me, you know." I rub my tender arm.

"Serves you right for running off like you did." Scott looks over at Barris and Nolan, still glued by the window. "Who's that?"

Nolan clears his throat and steps forward. "My name is Dr. Davic Nolan."

Scott's eyebrows knit together, his frown deepening. "Who?"

I whistle at Nolan and point to the loft. He nods. "I can explain who I am and catch you all up to speed on Cragen if you'll allow me." Nolan doesn't wait for anyone to agree. He saunters back up to the loft full of depressing files. Emmett, Scott, Jacklyn, Rylie and

Kade follow while Barris continues to stand guard by the window. I stick to the back, Dylan close behind.

But as we reach the steps, Dylan stops me with a hard hand on my elbow.

"Can I talk to you for a minute?" he asks, his tone dark and husky.

I nod sadly and sit on the bottom step. I can faintly hear Nolan jump into the story of his involvement with the experiments. Honestly, I'd rather have Dylan yell at me for the next ten minutes than listen to that horror story again.

"Are you okay?" he begins, surprisingly calm.

I hesitate. "Yes?"

"Oh, good…" he smacks my arm. "What the *hell*?! You just left without saying anything? Did you really think you'd get far without anyone noticing?"

I don't say anything.

"Seriously, Kiaya? What the hell was going through your mind? Did you really think you could prevent us from coming after you? Did you honestly believe you could face Cragen alone? That I would just *let* you face him alone?"

My eyes sting. I blink it away. "You done?"

"No, I –" Dylan pauses, eyes bright with fear as he takes a deep breath.

"Why do you care, huh?" I stand abruptly, a little too close for comfort, but I hold my ground. "Why come after me if I made you so mad?"

His voice comes out calmer this time, yet still firm. "Oh, Kaiya. Don't you remember what I said back at the farmhouse?"

I shake my head.

His mood shifts considerably as our eyes lock, perhaps because he can see the frustration behind my teary eyes. The corner of his mouth twitches as he reaches to tuck a loose strand of hair behind my ear. Even with this simple gesture, Dylan's careful to avoid too much contact. Maybe I was wrong. Maybe he *did* feel the shock before.

"I told you I wouldn't come along just to let you run into fire. And I meant it."

And I can suddenly tell by the gold smile in his eyes that he does mean it. For some unexplainable reason, this man would risk his neck – like his previously mangled foot – to help me.

I smile at him. He cups my face in his hand, and the electric shock is replaced by a pleasant warmth and slight jolt, almost like the rush you feel when jumping from a cliff into a body of water. Your heart stops for a moment, then the thrill ignites your every nerve. You're suddenly hyperaware that you're flying while also oblivious to everything else around you. Yes, just like that, only with more anxiety. I take a shaky breath and lean into his touch.

"I hope so."

"Better know so."

And he kisses me.

It isn't an urgent kiss, but I can feel weeks of holding back now releasing under his lips, as if he's saying all the things he's wanted to say since our first encounter without ever uttering a word. Dylan cups his other hand to the other side of my face and presses his lips harder to mine, yet the kiss remains slow and gentle. He's breathing new life into me, one where the past never existed, my worries have all but disintegrated under his hands and I can just be there with him. It lasts so long that I start to feel dizzy, like I'm in a dream where I'm about to collapse and fall into nothingness before I wake up to a painful reality.

And that's when I realize what I'm doing. What *we* are doing, and why it's wrong despite everything finally feeling right. I'm a ticking time-bomb, after all. And I can't take him out with me. So, I have to be the one to pull away.

We just stand there for a moment, forehead to forehead, listening to each other's breathing. It's a tad bit embarrassing, because my breathing is shaky and my heart thuds unevenly in my ears. He doesn't seem to notice, though.

I step back and sigh with defeat.

"What is it?"

I laugh, a nervous noise that doesn't match the anxious knot in my gut. "You know, you were right this whole time?"

"I usually am, but what about this time?"

"Your theory about experimentation," I say, eyes on the floor as I speak. "You were right. Your nightmares about Cragen experimenting on me, and about what he's going to do when he finds us...your crazy theory was right."

"Why do you say that? What do you mean, Kaiya?" His brows pull together, confusion evident in the creases.

I point up the stairs as I sit down. "Dr. Nolan is explaining right now exactly what I mean. You better go join them."

Dylan hesitates, eyeing me suspiciously.

"I'll still be here when he's done," I reassure him.

Dylan puts a hand on my shoulder and squeezes gently before stepping around me to join the unpleasant conversation in the loft. Though subtle, the touch leaves a sting behind.

In an effort to distract myself, I make the snap-decision to ransack the place. There isn't much to take except gurney sheets and some scalpels. I can't even bring myself to touch the surgical tools. How pathetic is that?

Upon further exploration, I discover a door on the west wall leading to a gray room no bigger than a water closet. The room is empty, aside from four sets of manacles, one set mounted on each wall, and a singular wooden chair screwed to the floor's center. I wonder briefly how much of my time was spent in this room before I was transferred to another building. Who shared this room with me? How many of its occupants are still alive?

Barris emerges in the creaky doorway and releases a low whistle.

"Forgot this room existed, to be honest," he says, leaning one arm on the frame. I can tell he's thinking about whoever he'd saved from this room. I'm sure Dylan has been in here, too. If the walls could speak…

"Hmm," is all I can say.

"You good?"

"I guess. You?"

"Never better." Barris flashes a too casual smile.

"I wanted to come here to get answers," I say slowly, unable to completely level with my cousin. Barris would recognize the pain in my eyes and most likely do something rash. That, or he would try to ease my anxiety with some awkward display in an effort to get me to laugh. When I finally work up the courage to look at him, I'm pleasantly surprised by the lack of interest on his face. I clear my throat ineptly. "I got my answers. Now what do we do?"

"The answer to that is pretty simple, isn't it?" Now it's his turn not to look at me.

"What's that, exactly?"

"Kill Cragen, of course."

I gulp. "You say that as if it would be so easy."

"It should be. With all the pain and death, he has caused, it should be no big thing to end it." The flame in Barris' eyes darkens, his jaw taut. "But I know from experience that it won't be easy to live with. And that needs to be your call."

As much as I resent Cragen for what he's done, for the time I've lost, for the toxicity lurking in my veins, for the threat he poses to my friends, my family, myself, for the endless nightmares I have no doubt he has somehow inflicted upon me, for the near-death experiences, for the literal deaths, for the loss of my memories and my identity...does any of this justify killing a person? Is this longing for revenge rationalized?

"Surely there's another answer. Another way."

Barris shrugs. "When you come up with this magical solution, let me know." And he saunters back to his post.

The 'meeting' must have adjourned because the stairs are overcome with rapid stomping. I lean in the terror room doorway and watch as Jacklyn rushes to my side and flings herself at me. My returned hug is awkward in nature but feels like the correct response. She holds on for too long, smothering my face in her strawberry locks. I can't see through them, but I know the others are waiting there.

"Cragen will pay for this," Scott growls from a distance.

Jacklyn, still holding me, agrees. "With my fist to his face." She releases me. The others stand in a circle close by. Jacklyn moves to join them.

"So, what now?" Rylie wonders aloud. "We wait for him to show up and try to convince him to stop?"

"That's not going to work," Emmett says. "Doc said Cragen's gone psycho."

Nolan scrunches his nose like he wants to argue then shrugs. "More or less. His brain has been compromised too much to see reason."

"Maybe we should just run," Kade suggests shyly. "Flee the state. Go somewhere he won't find Kaiya."

The debate continues without me as I slide into the background. Dylan joins me.

"Kaiya, I am so sorry."

"Nolan explain everything?"

"Yes. Are you okay?"

"Been better," is all I say.

Tension expands thick enough to slice and serve à la mode.

I try to concentrate on a game plan despite the fuzz in my head. Eventually, we're going to run into Cragen, no matter how hard we try to avoid him. Then what? Nolan made it clear Cragen isn't above bloodshed, but are we? How far is this going to go before I take matters into my own hands?

"Please say something."

So, I do. "We need to find Cragen."

"Let's not be hasty," Dylan says. "We find him, or he finds us, you know what will happen. Do you really want to take that chance? Are you willing to let someone die for it?" I wince, then he quickly adds, "What if something happens? Do you really want that nightmare to come true?"

"I don't really give a damn what happens to me," I snap quietly. "When I find Cragen, I *will* kill him. He will pay for what he's done. I will do it to protect the only family I have left. To protect Scott and Jacklyn and Rylie and *you.*"

"And what about you?" he demands in a soft voice. "What about me?"

And in front of us, in a totally different yet similar conversation:

"We could use her as bait," Emmett suggests. "Make Cragen come to her, and when the time is right, we take him out."

"Are you insane?" Scott yells. "We can't!"

"We can't do that, man," Rylie agrees to my surprise "She is our friend. We're not using her as bait."

"She's just going to die soon anyway," Nolan mutters, then slaps a hand over his mouth.

"He has a point," I holler. Dylan backhands my shoulder, a sound of utter disgust and disbelief creeps from his throat. I ignore him, peal myself from the doorway and join the planning circle.

"Cragen needs to be stopped," Barris joins, too. "What other choice do we have?"

"Other than giving up and handing her over," Nolan mutters. Again, he claps a palm to his mouth like the frightened little man he is.

190

Of course, that remark starts an uproar. So many voices at once. I can't decipher what's being said, or who's even talking! After a minute of shouting, things calm down, and everyone waits for me to say something. But what do I say? My tongue feels like a sponge in my mouth.

"I just don't think hunting him down is a good idea," Kade offers in a small voice.

"I still say we should use you as bait to lure him out," Emmett says.

I clap my hands together. "I'm in. What's the plan?"

"Kaiya," Dylan protests.

I spin around in irritation. "If you don't approve, you don't have to be here."

"Fine," he says through gritted teeth. "But only because I'm not going to watch you kill yourself."

Dylan storms off out the window.

I sigh.

"He'll be fine," Rylie says. "He's just stubborn."

I nod. "Think you could go check on him? Maybe talk a little sense into him?"

"I can *try*," he says, and follows in his brother's footsteps.

While listening to the boys argue audibly outside about my poor judgement, Barris suggests going back to the place where Blair and the mongrils held me hostage to 'make the trade.' He even makes a little diagram on one of the gurneys using scraps of cloth and surgical tools (which, again, makes me cringe internally).

"Cragen will be on his way here when he figures out you didn't follow Nolan's fake trail," Barris says.

191

"We 'accidently' plant a trail to make him think we're going back to the community, then create a new path for them to follow going into the old factory building. Maybe we're using it for a pretend rest stop. I dunno. Anyway, we leave Kaiya out in the open. The rest of us can hide in the trees or wherever and wait for him. Then, when we have a clear shot...*Bang*! It is over. She's safe from psycho, we're safe from impending doom. We all go home."

I have to admit it isn't a bad plan despite the lack of details. My dear cousin is more cunning than I've given him credit for. Or at least I think so, until he tries to snatch my blade from me. I'd been twirling it in my hand while we discussed my part in the plan. After a second of struggle, he manages to take it from me.

"Hey!" I exclaim. My empty fingers sting a little.

"You can't have any weapons on you," he says, stabbing it into the gurney mattress for no reason other than legal destruction of property. "You're the bait, remember?"

"You can't really expect her to go through with this without any protection," Scott protests.

"No, he's right," I say. Admitting so tastes strange on my tongue. "That would just be more weapons in Cragen's hands. We don't want that."

Jacklyn clears her throat randomly.

"Hey guys," she says, concern creeping into her petite voice. "The guys have been out there a while, don't you think?"

Everyone falls silent. I can't hear their faint yet familiar arguing anymore. In fact, I can't hear anything. It's too quiet.

"Shit."

I charge the window and jump through, rounding the corner of the compound to have an arrow shot at my feet.

Chapter 17

The arrow missed my shoe, but only by a hair.

Whoever the shooter is, he or she must be a wonderful shot. The tip slid through one of the loops on my shoelace and pierced the dirt a centimeter from my sole. I don't dare to bend over and yank it out, especially not while I can feel several armed people with their weapons poised on me.

I look up slowly, hands in the air, and immediately wish I were in one of my nightmares.

Yes, it had been my plan to find and kill Cragen.

But I didn't know I'd be standing in front of him so soon, baring no weapon to defend myself, while his mongrils hold the noisy brothers hostage.

"Hello, hello!" His familiar booming voice rips through my ears. I turn unwillingly towards the sound.

Twenty men in an untidy row – they've been waiting there for us for god-knows how long. They're all armed with handguns and bows, arrows pointed and ready – and at the end of the row he stands, hands on his hips, a revolver hanging loosely from his pointer finger on his left side. His blond hair and familiar scarred face give away his identity. Or is it the suppressed memories together that gives him away? Or the way that he stares at me now, eyes ablaze with God-knows-what. Old love? Lust? Bloodlust? Jealousy? Resentment? Nostalgia? Maybe just insanity?

Cragen flashes an evil grin, one that boils my core. How my palm itches to slap that stupid grin from his face. "There she is the woman of the hour. My, my, how different you look! It's been entirely too long."

I clench my fists at my sides, glaring up at him. Cragen whistles down the row of men, and the two restraining Dylan and Rylie push them forward and shove them to their knees. Dylan raises his head slowly, eyes on me.

Cragen holds a single hand in the air. I turn to see that he's motioning to my friends, who have joined us outdoors, to stay put. Once I twist back to look at Cragen, he saunters over. My shoulders tense as he stops just a foot from me, so close that I smell his bitter, diseased breath. He looks me over carefully. Too carefully. If it weren't for the twenty other men ready to shoot, I would punch him for eyeing me this way. His smile turns crooked.

"I should have given you more credit. When I sent my people to get you, I figured you would be easy pickings. Yet you've escaped and managed to make it this far. Didn't know what I was dealing with. I guess you're stronger than I remember." And yet, his voice is colored thickly with…is that sarcasm? An inside joke? Or is he just happy to see me? Blech.

I say nothing. I stand perfectly still and stare past him. He begins to circle me, pausing to tuck a loose strand of hair behind my ear. I shudder. His touch is cold and unforgiving. He then traces my shoulder blades with his fingertips. My knuckles burn with the urge to hit him.

Dylan watches Cragen begrudgingly and finally snaps. He rips his hands from the mongril and whips out his pocketknife – *they really forgot to search him*? But before he advances, Cragen wraps a swift arm around my shoulders and pulls me against him, a large combat knife to my throat. Dylan freezes, but he doesn't lower his weapon.

"Come any closer and I'll slice her open."

"You wouldn't," Dylan calls his bluff through gritted teeth. "You need her."

"Yes, but I can make her wish she were dead," Cragen threatens. I flinch as he cuts me a little, warm blood trickling down my neck.

Cragen is bluffing, of course, but after seeing the blood run across my skin, Dylan loses his valor. "Okay, okay." He drops the knife.

"Good," Cragen says, pulling his knife away from me slightly. I must've held my breath because I gasp for air once the metal blade frees me. One mongril steps forward to stand behind Dylan – wait, is that *Blair*? Yep, it's Blair. The wind blows her hair back just enough to reveal butterfly strips along the gash Dylan put on her face. She grins at me as if to say *karma's a bitch*.

Dylan doesn't look at either of them. He watches Cragen and I. I attempt to relax my expression to show him I'm okay, but I'm paralyzed. Dylan wears fear and anger proudly on his sleeve, and Cragen finds it to be humorous.

196

"You look oddly familiar," Cragen comments. "Where have I seen you before?...Oh yes, it was after our raid on that Amish-looking community. You've been here before. Now I remember. The one who wouldn't scream. Hmmm…"

Out of the corner of my eye, I see the others gawking at us. I turn my head slightly and shoot them a pleading look. *Do something! Anything!* But honestly, what can they do? Cragen's men outnumber us. They have us at gunpoint – well, arrow-point. Cragen has me. There isn't really anything they can do. Nothing I can ask of them.

Cragen tightens his grip on me. I'm forced to look forward again.

Rylie coughs, loud and wet. I'm pulled out of my fear for a brief moment to look at him. I hadn't noticed the blood seeping from him a moment ago.

Rylie has an open wound – knife wound? It's too wide to be from an arrow or bullet – on the left side of his collar. Half of his shirt is soaked. He coughs again, groans, cringes his shoulders forward like he has the urge to hold his wound, but his pinned arms prevent him from doing so.

"Your brother doesn't look so good." Cragen throws his chin towards Rylie. "You should probably get him taken care of. We won't disturb you."

Dylan doesn't move.

"Dylan," I finally speak in a soft voice. Cragen instinctively raises the blade higher and closer to me. I try my best to ignore his scare tactic, lifting my chin away from his weapon. I clear my throat quietly so my voice will be even. "Go take care of Rylie."

Dylan still doesn't budge.

"I would listen to her if I were you," Cragen sings.

Jaw clench. Still no movement.

Cragen sighs dramatically, carefully curling over to stand at my side. "What a pity. I guess you'll just have to come with us, then, won't you?" In my peripheral, I see his smile twist up to his ears, and he lets out a low, creepy chuckle. His bloodshot eyes have tiny streaks of purple at the corners. He looks crazy! Scary insane!

Dr. Nolan is right. He has completely lost his mind.

He stops chuckling abruptly and whistles.

Blair grabs Dylan by the elbows. Cragen grabs my arms with one hand, knife still poised in the other. The mongrils all step forward and await orders. We all turn towards the compound.

But Cragen freezes at the sight of my friends.

No, at the sight of *Barris*.

Barris narrows his eyes on Cragen but makes no move.

A savage sound escapes Cragen, like that of an infected. He releases me, only for his arms to be replaced by a mongril's, and stomps over to Barris. The rest of the mongrils follow, motioning with their arrows and gun barrels for the others to back away. With no other choice, they back up to the wall, leaving Barris several yards away with Cragen right in his face.

Cragen takes a loud breath and exhales it in Barris' face.

"Ohhhh, I've been waiting a loooong time for this, you murderous son-of-a-bitch."

Barris snickers, but his face remains flat.

"What's so funny?"

"Like it's any different from what you've been doing. Tell me though, how are Ma and Pa?" Barris speaks, eyes still burning into Cragen's.

And everything goes quiet. You could hear a pen drop with this tension!

Cragen huffs out a curt laugh. His hand comes to Barris' shoulder and squeezes.

Then he plunges his knife into Barris' gut.

My ears buzz from the screaming, but I can still hear Barris suck in a pained mouthful before fisting Cragen's shirt. Cragen rips the knife from one end to the other, then Barris collapses. His guts don't just fall out. No, we see no string of intestines or other organs as people would commonly believe to see when a person is slashed this way. Only blood. Redder than I've ever seen come from a person.

Eyes blur over, stomach twists, head still hammered with the screaming. It's not until my throat rubs raw from the sound that I realize the screams are my own. Yet Barris makes no noise, aside from the gut-wrenching heaves as he clutches his torn stomach.

Cragen towers over him, despite my pleas for him to stop.

"Still not enough," he says. "No. You, my friend, deserve far worse than this. I think that's only fair." He looks up and snaps his fingers. "Bows, here. Guns, stay."

The bowmen surround Cragen and crumpled Barris. Gunmen hold my anxious friends still.

"This is for my parents," Cragen says, then he flees the circle.

A hailstorm of arrows rain on Barris. I can't watch, though I continue to plead. My eyes burn, my throat burns, my chest tightens. *Barris is lost.* My knees give out. The mongril has to hold me up.

This is what I asked for.

He's lost because of me.

Jacklyn, Scott, Emmett, and an injured Rylie watch with torched visages as Dylan and I are towed back to the building. Kade cowers beside them, focused on Barris' body looking like a porcupine. But no Nolan in sight. *Where's Nolan?*

****

"What?! What do you want from me?!"

I'm stuck yet again in my nightmare, now too real. Barris has died again, and I've cried over his dead body for an eternity. My personal hell has become real. This has already happened. So why am I dreaming about it now?

His eyes fly open, as they have before in my last dream. He stares up at me with an accusatory scowl. He knows as well as I that his death is my fault. He stands, arrows still protruding from him as if he were a pin cushion. He hobbles towards me. I tumble back. *What is he going to do? Give me what I deserve?*

I back right into Scott. Jacklyn. Emmett. Kade. Rylie. Nolan. They're all dead, yet they swarm me, just like before.

A warm hand on my shoulder. Dylan. He is dead, too.

His throat has been slashed again with a jagged blade. The front of his shirt is still soaked in crimson. Face still bruised and broken.

The others still stand in a circle around us. Everyone smiles, just like before, despite the fact that they're clearly dead.

Dylan offers his hand. I take it, still a sobbing, shaking mess.

"Did I do this?"

No answer.

"Are you *all* dead because of me?"

Still no answer, just smiles.

"I'm so sorry, I didn't mean to…"

But I *did* mean to. I wanted revenge. I knew I shouldn't, but I plotted it anyway. Now Barris is gone, and everyone else is doomed because of my insistent bloodlust.

I only just got him back in my life. Things were finally making sense. I finally had a fraction of a family, someone to understand my motives, to accept me without explanation.

My cousin is *dead* because of me. Dead. Lost. Gone. Never coming back. My only surviving relative slaughtered by the sick and sadistic. And I let it happen. Now it will happen to every last one of us, starting with more experimentation on me.

They continue to smile. I continue to freak out. *Why are they smiling?!*

Barris is the first to speak this time. "It wasn't your fault, Kaiya. None of this was your fault."

"But it is," I cry out. "I'm the reason Cragen killed you."

Everyone in the circle shakes their heads in synchronization.

201

Barris frowns. "I did this. I killed his parents. I finally reaped what I sowed. You didn't do any of this."

Then Dylan steps forward. "No. Cragen did this."

Then Jacklyn. "You have to stop him."

"How? How do I stop him?"

None of them answer. The three steps back into the circle.

And Barris disappears, like wind whisking away the fog.

Only the living stand before me, blood and injuries gone. Scott, Kade, Rylie, Jacklyn, Emmett, Dr. Nolan, and most importantly Dylan. The blood is gone from his white shirt. His bruises have disappeared. His throat is unscathed.

"No one else has to die, Kaiya," Scott said.

"No one else," Jacklyn repeats.

The dream doesn't end abruptly like my previous dreams. It gradually fades out, like I'm being pulled away from the dark room into a brighter one.

I keep my eyes shut under the strange new light.

Chapter 18

When I come to, Cragen towers over me and holds my left eyelid open while shining a small flashlight at me. Blink, blink. Jerk my head to the side. But I can't roll away. I'm strapped down to one of the gurneys. Vile rises to my throat as I struggle. No one else in the room with us. Just me and Cragen.

"Wakey," he says. He sits back and gestures to the room. "Now, isn't this nostalgic?"

Of course, he would confuse my horror for nostalgia.

"I really wouldn't know," I spit.

"Oh, right. No memories. My bad."

"What are you going to do to me?"

"Nothing yet," he sighs. "We moved all our equipment from this place to a new location, aside from a few scalpels and pliers. I just want to do a quick examination before we get going."

"Why?"

"Because I haven't seen you in two and a half years. Gotta make sure everything is still intact." Cragen smiles wickedly, then looks me over. He starts with my arms and stops when he reaches the scarred bite mark.

"I thought you were dead, you know," he says in a casual tone. "We got back to the building and found infected snacking on a corpse. I naturally assumed it was you, and that coward Nolan managed to get the others free and left you behind. Man, it was rough for a couple of years. I couldn't figure out why my experiments were failing, why I couldn't recreate your perfect morus cells.

"It wasn't until several months ago that they found you alive. My men were wondering the streets in search of more test subjects, and they brought back a drawing. It was a strange sketch of a beautiful sleeping girl with wavy hair and freckles…the same button nose as you…" he clears his throat and continues. "Of course, I recognized it was you right away. Your friend is one hell of an artist. So, I sent my men out to find patient 33. And –"

"And you found her sketchbook, and now you've found *me*," I interrupt. "So, what's your plan here? You killed my cousin, my last surviving relative. You gonna kill me too?"

"He wasn't your last surviving relative."

He wasn't?

But I'm too panicked to ask about that at this moment. So, I ask: "What are you going to do with me now?"

Cragen's eyes flicker to the gray room to my right, then back to me. "I'm glad you asked. Now that you've clearly blossomed, I need to finish what I've started. And to do that, I'm going to need a few samples of your blood. Maybe even run a few…tests.

But before I do that…" Cragen stands and rushes to the gray room. He returns pushing a rollie chair where Dylan sits, tied, and gagged.

How long had I been blacked out? A purple swell has replaced Dylan's right eye, and a small cut lays delicately on his cheekbone. He spots me and murmurs against the gag and duct tape.

"Now," Cragen says. "This young lad has a weak strand of morus created from my cells. I didn't get the chance to examine the healing progress, as his brother so rudely removed him. Maybe if I do a few quick tests on *him* and adjust my hypothesis, we can dispose of this one and properly move forward."

Dispose of him?

Cragen turns to grab a scalpel. He murmurs something to himself about it being '*not big enough.*' He looks around for a moment, spots the knife Barris had taken from me earlier protruding from a nearby gurney, and yanks it out.

I speak quickly, hysteria easing into my voice. "You're wasting your time. You don't need to run any *tests* on him. That's what I'm here for. Let's just get this over with."

Dylan scowls at me.

Cragen lets out a *Bah!* and moves to the foot of my bed.

"But we've got some unfinished business," he growls, glaring at Dylan as he struggles against his restraints. "Even more so now, it seems."

"What do you mean?"

"I mean, I know *exactly* what's going on here," he motions between Dylan and I with the tip of the blade. "And if you think I'm going to let this go just because we've been apart for a few years," he laughs manically, "you couldn't be more wrong."

"Seriously?" I shout. "*Seriously*? A – I don't even remember the time we spent together because *someone* took my memories from me after performing some *sick* experiments. And B – He has nothing to do with this. You want to torture me? I'm right here. What the hell are you waiting for? It's time to let him go and face me."

Admittedly, I didn't expect this boldness to rise from me, as my tone doesn't waver as much as I anticipated. Dylan's struggles intensify, his mutters crescendo to undecipherable pleas and threats.

Cragen steps around to my left side again and reaches out to stroke my cheek. I turn my head away instinctively, grinding my teeth.

"All in due time, dear," he says.

Then he advances on Dylan.

But just as he stabs Dylan in the shoulder – precisely in the same spot Rylie was stabbed – and Dylan cries out, Nolan jumps out of hiding and smashes something ceramic over Cragen's head.

Had he been hiding in here this whole time?

Cragen crumbles. Dylan huffs in pain. Nolan huffs with adrenaline.

But the victory is short-lived as mongrils rush in. Chaos ensues.

I blackout when I was hit with the butt stroke of a rifle.

I'm in the woods again, rope binding me to a tree trunk. The bark scratches at my back as I struggle, but I can't free my wrists. The rope won't budge.

And then the yelling starts, followed by gunshots and arrows zipping past to stab aimlessly in the dirt. I can't see around the massive trunk.

Jacklyn runs past. She's gunned down.

Then Rylie. Arrow to the back.

Scott runs by, followed by Emmett and Kade and Nolan. They don't stop to examine our dead friends.

How did none of them notice me? I try to yell for help, but they don't stop. Just like every other nightmare before, my screams have made no sound. But did they not see me? Did they not see our fallen friends?

And then Dylan barrels past me. I pointlessly scream to him again.

He stops.

Takes a long pause to stare at me with tortured eyes.

And runs after my friends.

He isn't gunned down. He doesn't die. He just runs off into the distance, fading into the hazy cherry-velvet sunset. He's leaving me behind.

The mongrils follow my companions until they are but melting stick figurines. Their rabid cackles turn to desperate cries, and they drop one by one.

It's just me. I'm all alone. The ground smothers the light, velvet smoke fades. Darkness swallows me.

****

"Have you taken a sample yet?"

"No, sir."

"Well hurry up and get on it! We don't have much time to test this."

I try my best not to move. That's not hard. My legs are stiff and tingling with numbness. Something cold holds my wrists above me. There's a thudding in my head, like someone wacked me with a baseball bat. Where am I? It must be an open space, because the male voices I hear seem to echo from across the area.

That's when I remember Cragen stabbing Dylan, Nolan knocking Cragen unconscious, and the rifle that did the same to me. What happened to Dylan and the others? Did the mongrils kill them? My mind swims with worry.

"Have you seen the hot plate?" I don't recognize this voice.

"I think it's upstairs. Should be under the bed floorboard with the other chemicals." Unmistakably Cragen.

"I'll go get it, then."

"I'll come with. I need to check on the boy anyway."

What boy? Who are they talking about?

Stomp, stomp, stomp. Then the door clicks shut. I can't fake unconsciousness any longer. I open my eyes slowly, and suddenly wish I hadn't.

This must be the new compound location Cragen spoke about. It looks like something taken straight out of a horror story. I'm facing the side of the stairs. Under the staircase are hand-built shelves, one for each stair. They're lined with rows of test tubes, beakers, and tiny bottles containing various liquids. The seventh shelf down is longer, thicker, and covered in papers and tools like a workbench. On the highest shelf is a row of red vials. I squint, concentrating on the labels. It's a little blurry, but I'm able to make some of the labels out – *Thank you, heightened senses.* The two vials on the left read 'Mr. Jones' and 'Mrs. Jones.' Next to those are the names of my friends, followed by one labeled 'Amish boy.' Beside them is the only empty vial on that row. It reads 'Kaiya,' marked with a little red heart on the tail of the 'y.' About three yards to the right from where I'm pinned to the wall by metal cuffs is a stained queen-sized mattress – *was that there before?* – with two corpses. I don't recognize either of them, but they have slashes all over their bodies. Were they infected?

Gotta be a nightmare, right? I squeeze my eyes shut, then wrench them back open. *Why am I not waking up?* I try again. Nope. Still dreaming. I struggle desperately against my cuffs and pray it's just another twisted nightmare…that I'll wake up any minute. *Come on! Wake up! Wake up!* I throw my head against the wall. *Wake up!* But I'm greeted only by a sting on the back of my head. No doubt a knot will form.

I'm not sleeping. I realize with a painful throbbing in my skull that this is real. I'm really trapped in his basement.

I start to hyperventilate. I know exactly what he'll do to me. What he'll do to *them* after he's through with me. And there's no way for me to stop it now. Nothing I can do. I'm trapped. And Cragen will give everyone the morus cells that will slowly drive them to insanity and death. And I won't be able to stop him.

Calm down, my conscience whispers. Everything is going to be fine. You're overreacting.

But am I? No one's coming to save me. I'm not even sure my friends are still alive. Even if Dylan or Rylie or Scott or Jacklyn do come to my rescue,

Cragen will kill them. He likely won't hesitate again. No one will stand in his way. Unless they sneak past Cragen, but how easy would that be? I haven't the faintest idea how many of his men are here with him.

My thoughts are interrupted by advancing footsteps overhead. The basement door creaks open. I see a pair of combat boots coming down the stairs, followed by a pair of old worn tennis shoes.

Cragen rounds the corner of the last step to approach me, his boots creating a dull echoing thud with each stride. His 'sidekick' follows, head bent over a clipboard, never acknowledging us. He doesn't look like a mongril. Is he new? Has he not been submitted to Cragen's 'studies' yet? Cragen looks up at me and smiles, crossing his arms over his chest. He breathes out a long, pleased sigh.

"Kiaya," he says my name like it fills the empty spot where his heart should be. His voice sends shock waves down my spine. His eyes scan my body as if he's doing a routine assessment but seem to drag over me. I want to recoil from him. It's impossible to shrink away, though, being held against the wall. I'm thankful for the space between us. "So strong and sturdy. Your years of healing have done you well."

"Cragen," I say curtly. "What a displeasure. Where are my friends?"

"How sassy. Is that how you greet an old friend?"

"I'm sure you forfeited that title a long time ago."

"Not like you would actually remember it," he says. He cockily steps forward. I spit in his face. "Still quite the spit-fire, I see." He wipes my saliva off his scrunched-up nose. "No matter. We can catch up while I complete a few trials."

Cragen and his assistant spin away from me, pouring over a pile of papers on the workbench.

"Have you had much discomfort since your healing?" Cragen asks too casually over his shoulder.

I don't respond.

"I asked you a question, Kaiya."

I still don't respond. He turns to glare at me, to force me to cave. I glare back, still silent.

"Have you fought any infected yet?"

No reply.

"I'm assuming by the claw marks on you that you have. How many were there? Did you fight them alone? Was it difficult?"

No reply. I narrow my eyes at him.

"How about Dylan? Does he fight well?"

"Leave him out of this," I snarl.

"That's all it took, huh?" he grins a wicked grin.

I don't answer, my lips pressed into a hard line.

"He's not coming, dearest," he says in a pseudo-sympathetic voice. "He's feeling a little...under the weather." Cragen laughs darkly.

The urge to threaten Cragen burns my mouth. I bite my tongue.

"Don't worry, he's not alone. He's all safe and sound next door. I have a few friends of mine guarding him. I'm afraid he won't be able to make it over here."

I can't look at him anymore. I feel the anger visible on my cheeks. I focus instead on one of the bottle labels.

Cragen turns back to his papers, muttering to the other man about things that need to be prepared.

I finally can't help it anymore. Questions burn inside of me like a flat iron down my throat. I speak to him despite my strategic silence.

"I saw the picture you had in the loft."

"And you smashed it," he calls over his shoulder. "I don't have any frames to replace that."

"Tell me why."

He sighs and turns around, taking three slow steps towards me.

"Why what? Why I have a picture of us? I thought it was rather obvious. Because I care about you. I always have."

Disgust lingers in my voice. "If you care about me so much, then why are you doing this? Why are you so eager to do this?"

"This isn't about you and me anymore. The fate of the world depends on your sacrifice."

I cringe at the last word. "You're insane."

"You may think that, but I know this is the right thing to do. And I am sorry." He strokes my cheek again. I recoil from his hand as if it is a jellyfish stinger. I want to argue with him and plead for my release, but I know it will do no good. He may be vocally unchallenged, but he's far too gone to see reason.

Cragen turns again to his papers, pulling out a microscope and small glass slide with a red dot in the center. After a few minutes of *oooo*-ing and *ahhhh*-ing, he picks up a needle. From what I can see from behind, he appears to be poking at something on the slide. It's frustrating him. He curses repeatedly under his breath after a couple of pokes.

"Why isn't it working, sir?" the assistant finally speaks in a small shaky voice.

Cragen throws the tiny poking needle at the wall. It ricochets and clinks to the floor. The assistant flinches as if Cragen had thrown a frying pan at him. Why's he so scared?

"I'm pretty sure," Cragen speaks through gritted teeth, "the cells need to have something to fight off, or a host to protect. They can't repair themselves without a damaged vessel." He spins towards me, his face twisted with a strange mixture of sympathy and anticipation.

He digs out his pocketknife and draws closer. I shrink into the wall. Nowhere to run, nowhere to turn, no way to defend myself. "I truly am sorry, but this is strictly for scientific purposes. I have to know what will happen. Our humanity depends on this."

"What will happen if what?" I ask, my jaw clenched tight to hide the instability in my voice. I don't take my eyes off the knife.

"This may hurt a little," he mutters.

His knuckles pull tight on his hand, ash white against the black hilt. He takes a sudden jagged breath and slashes out at me.

My throat is dry and rough. I guess screaming for an hour straight does strain the vocal cords.

I take it surprisingly well the first time he cuts me. He slashes my upper arm open, the cut jagged, an inch deep and about half a foot in length. Blood oozes deeply, covering the inside of my elbow. The sharp sting makes me physically shudder. I bite my tongue and scream inwardly. The groaning is inevitable. I can't stop myself from making noise altogether, but I at least keep my mouth shut and put on a brave face. No tears. No begging. I refuse to give him an ounce of satisfaction.

Until he cuts me again.

The second slash is to my thigh. The knife slides deeper beneath my skin than it had before. The heavy burning sensation is unbearable, and easily cracks my composer. I squeeze my eyes shut – as if that'll counteract the stinging – and let out a pained screech, one I'm almost certain the mongrils and Dylan hear next door. Hot blood runs down the inside of my pant leg, matting the baggy jean material to my skin.

My pain enthuses Cragen. He's mad! This makes the torture even more frightening. He continues to slash at me, careful not to go as deep as he had before. I'd compare it to receiving hundreds of paper cuts, except more serious and much more agonizing.

Through the fuzzy throbbing in my head, I attempt to distract myself, but the longing for answers can't be silenced. What good will I be if I bleed to death? Why not torture me in a less wasteful manner? Did it start out as an experiment and turn into some sort of release for him? Like crossing business with pleasure? Is this part of the madness? And why doesn't he just take my blood and be done with it? Why go through the extra tests? Unless…

After the hour's up and my voice is so hoarse that I can't scream anymore, Cragen finally stops. He wipes the knife clean on his jeans, closes it, and stows it back in his pocket. He looks up at me apologetically.

"Don't worry, you'll be fine," he said. "I wouldn't have done it if it weren't absolutely necessary to record all possible results." Cragen then holds a tiny bottle under my nose, one with a silver, shimmery looking substance in it. "Do you know what this is?"

I don't answer. Mainly because I physically can't. Not without it hurting.

"It's your morus cells. I withdrew two vials from you this morning. One to test the strength of the cells currently in your body, and –" he shakes the bottle in my face. "– one to *enhance* the strand. Now that I know what your cells can handle from the last time I had you with me, it's time to put the enhanced cells to the test."

Enhanced?!

As if the potentially deadly morus cells weren't enough, he's went and *enhanced* them?

I watch dreadfully as Cragen fills a needle with the silver fluid. It takes half the bottle to fill the syringe.

"You see, it started out as me finding a way to rid you of illness," he explains, but doesn't quite meet my eyes. "My parents got a little carried away with the project, I'll admit, but their intensions were good." I make a scoffing noise. Cragen snaps his eyes to mine in a threatening manner, then continues. "But I met someone on the road, a young woman. She reminded me a lot of you. We spent about a month together. She granted me shelter," he gestures at the four walls with wide arms, backing up slightly as he does so, "and I protected her from infected. Fair trade. But then I noticed her getting sick. Just like the infected before they turn. Radiation."

"How do you know it was radiation?" I ask in a froggy voice.

He ignores my question. "Don't you get it?! She had never been bitten. She wasn't the vicinity of the bombs during the war. Yet, she was sick. She was dying. Then I realized, what if everyone left around here were dying, just like sweet Katrisa? The only way to cure her and everyone else was to find you and recreate a more advanced, more heavily concentrated version of the morus."

"You experimented on her, didn't you?" I demand. "You gave her your cells because you were afraid and that's why she got sick. That's why she died. You're the reason she's gone!"

A savage snarl escapes his mouth. He advances, syringe poised in one hand, his knife magically reappearing in the other. He brings it to my throat, then catches himself.

"Oh, that's right," I laugh. "You need me *alive*."

Cragen flashes a devilish half-smile. "Oh, I don't have to kill you to kill you." He then snaps his fingers. "Bring in the girl."

A moment later, the assistant drags down –

"Jacklyn!"

"Kaiya! You okay?"

I nod weakly to her, though it's not the truth. Every part of my body throbs.

"Is this the artist?" Cragen points to Jacklyn as she's lowered to her knees.

I don't respond.

But Jacklyn does.

"I am. Are you Doctor Psycho?"

"Oh-oh-oh!" he jeers at her. "I *like* this one. Such a shame."

One swift movement. He slices her throat.

Choking noise, wide eyes, every adventure, and near-death experience escaping through the droplets from her lashes and the gushing blood from her jugular.

I'm so shocked by the swiftness that I can't speak. I can only cry alongside her as she slinkies to the ground, color and life fading from her irises.

I wish I could jump out of these restraints and avenge her. Even more, I wish it were me, lying in front of her, last breath used to fill the air with final optimisms. Of the people I have sentenced to death in my quest for answers and revenge, I hoped it would never come to this. Yet here she is. I'm the reason she bleeds out, the reason Emmett will never get to hold her again, to save her ass from infected one last time, to tease her for being so damn hopeful in a world where the diseased run rampant. For the million times she's helped me through the nightmares that plague me, I've imagined a million ways to repay her kindness, a debt I will never get the opportunity to repay thanks to Cragen.

But it's my fault, too. And it's an impossible pill to swallow.

I sob noisily, unable to rip my eyes from her now still figure.

Until Cragen advances on me with the needle again.

"Let that be a lesson to you."

I cringe to the wall expectantly.

Cragen laughs at my reaction. "Don't worry sweetheart, *this* one isn't for you." He turns to his assistant, throws him the closed bottle, and says, "Put the girl away. The next one. Bring him to me."

Him? Who's him?

The assistant cringes before dragging Jacklyn's body to the closet on the far side of the basement. He then saunters back up the stairs and returns two minutes later, pushing someone along in front of him. The person wears a bloody shirt and muddy shoes. The assistant forces the person to his knees and removes the gunnysack from his head.

"Rylie, is it?" Cragen asks.

Rylie blinks, looks around the basement frantically. After his eyes adjust, he looks up at me, alarmed by my appearance. He doesn't even notice the fresh blood puddle he kneels in.

"You okay?" he asks. What a stupid question. Had it been Dylan, though, he would be freaking out, cursing, threatening Cragen...then probably killed for opening his mouth... I'm thankful for Rylie's calm demeanor.

I don't respond. After all, I was just forced to watch my best friend die. The ache in my chest severely outweighs my physical discomfort. However, each movement and heavy breath feels like a stab to my injured arm and leg. With each passing minute I grow fainter and dizzier.

"Tell me, Rylie," Cragen said, drawing the attention back to himself. "How old are you?"

"Twenty-one," Rylie answers honestly. God, I wish he would stay silent.

"And your brother? How old is he?"

"Does it matter?"

"Oh, this one's got an attitude. Kaiya, you have some interesting friends."

"Leave him out of this," I croak to Cragen. My eyes focus still on the syringe in his hand.

"I'm afraid that is out of the question," Cragen says with a smile. He grabs a fist full of Rylie's hair and jams the needle into his neck.

"NO!" I cry out as he pushes the plunger down. Rylie sits still, his eyes welling up and threatening to brim over. "Damn you! You stupid bastard!"

"I'm sorry Kaiya, but I need more than just one test subject," he justifies. He releases Rylie and comes over to do the same to me.

The needle is cold, but the liquid he pumps into my neck feels like magma in my veins. It gives me the insane urge to claw at my skin to cool the fire with outside air. I wonder if it feels different for Rylie. After all, the morus already in my blood gives me an unpredictable pain tolerance.

I stare at Rylie. He bites his lip, his teeth drawing blood, but other than that, he doesn't show any signs of pain. Maybe he will be okay.

"Oh, and I'm sorry for this next part," Cragen adds.

Before I process what's happening, Cragen has his knife out again. The assistant pulls Rylie up to his feet and jumps out of the way just as Cragen flings around and drives the knife deep in Rylie's gut and drags it to the left, just like he did to Barris.

Rylie gasps. His eyes widen. Cragen pulls the knife out just as Rylie places his hands over the wound and topples backwards.

"He will live if he is worthy," Cragen says, cleaning his knife once again. "The new cells should be able to heal him before he dies. Well, maybe."

"YOU BASTARD!" I scream at him. Tears flow freely down my face. I struggle against my restraints. I ignore the pain in my arm. "I swear I will kill you! I swear it! I'll kill you!"

Cragen crosses his arms. "Says the restrained prisoner. How you gonna kill me from up there?" He grins a wicked grin. Rylie curls up on his side, pale and bloody, clenching his lower abdomen.

He just lays there, crumbled in a mixture of his blood and Jacklyn's.

Just like before…Cragen snapped his fingers, and everyone fell.

My nightmares are coming true.

"Unfortunately, I will have to leave you both here." Cragen bends down to clasp a manacle over Rylie's wrist, fastening the other end to a metal beam. "I can't wait around for the results. I have things to do, people to see," he winks at me, as if I'm supposed to know what it means, and continues. "I hope your friend lives. This young man here," he points to his assistant, "will be recording what happens. I know, it's terribly rude not to introduce the two of you, but what's the point anyway? And we will meet again soon. I promise. So, before I go…"

Cragen stands up on his tiptoes so he can reach my face. I turn from him as far as the wall will allow as he closes in to kiss me on the cheek, his breath hot against my skin. I hold my breath, but still smell the bitterness escaping his lips.

"I will be back for you," he promises. I shiver. No doubt he will be.

Chapter 19

I hang there motionless for what feels like ages. The assistant lingers in the corner by the worktable, looking up every now and then to write on his clipboard.

And Rylie lays in front of me. He, too, does not move.

I try saying his name every few minutes, but he does not respond. About 99 percent sure he's dead.

I cry quietly to myself. It's completely my fault. Emmett and Dylan and the others will never forgive me for this, and I won't blame them.

If that tree would have crushed me…if the swarm of infected would have killed me in that hotel…if Cragen would have just snapped my neck before taking me hostage…

…Barris and Jacklyn and Rylie would be alive.

Their sister was gone. Now Rylie is gone. Dylan will be all alone. Without a family. And he will know it's my fault, as I do. *Wherever you are, forgive me. I'm sorry. It should have been me. I'm so sorry.*

After my eyes dry, I search the room for anything that'll help me escape. The least I can do for them now is protect their loved ones, though I'd like to take their bodies home for a proper burial. There's a toolbox in the corner of the room. I could use bolt cutters or a screwdriver or something to break free, but how would I get to them? I can't move!

Things are looking bleak. There's no way for me to break out. No way to save the others. No way to avenge Jacklyn and Rylie....

I look back to Rylie, guilt welling up in my eyes again until I notice that his wound looks different, smaller. I squint my eyes and lean forward as far as the restraints will allow. Through the sliced hole in his shirt is a visible mark, but it can't be any bigger than a scratch from a nail. Only moments ago, it was a bloody hole in his body. Now it is merely a scrape. How's that even possible?!

The morus!

The enhanced cells are *healing him!*

I suddenly remember my own injuries. Through the fog in my brain, I realize that I feel no pain. Glancing down at my body, I see nothing. My wounds are gone! The only sign there were injuries at all are the giant crimson stains on my clothes. A visible, long scar has replaced the gash on my arm. It looks like an old scar, healed white and stretched tight across the muscle.

If the morus cells are healing Rylie's injuries, is he alive?

"Rylie? Rylie? Rylie?"

"Quiet," the assistant warns. No authority colors his tone.

I ignore him. "Rylie? Can you hear me? Rylie?"

"Shut up," he warns again, looking up from his clipboard.

"Rylie? Wake up Rylie!"

The assistant drops the clipboard on the desk and stomps over to me, an uneasy grimace behind his hard scowl. "I said be quiet. Are you deaf?"

"Are you stupid?" I retort. "Do you even know what you're doing?"

Cragen's sidekick reaches up with a daring hand. The slap rings. "Shut up already. I'm trying to concentrate. One more word, and I will –"

"What? You'll do what?"

There's a loud snap of metal. I blink and suddenly, the assistant isn't in front of me anymore. He's slammed into the adjacent wall, Rylie's arm at his throat.

Rylie. He *is* alive!

"Free her," Rylie growls at the assistant. He looks bigger, impossibly so, and more intimidating than before. His eyes glow a little brighter with sparks of rage sprinkling the edges. He pushes his arm farther into the boy's larynx. The boy gasps and struggles to speak. Rylie slams his hand against the wall beside the boy's face. The boy shutters. Rylie repeats himself.

I've never seen Rylie this way, so revived and dangerous.

"I can't," he says.

"Why the hell not?"

"I don't have the key."

"Then you're of no use," Rylie raises his fist in the air.

"Wait, wait!" the assistant cringes, hands up in defense. He reaches down with one shaking hand to retrieve a small key from his pocket.

Rylie rips it from his fingers. "Thanks." Rylie releases him, and points for the door. "Now go."

"Wait!" I say. Rylie grabs the boy by the back of his collar. "You can't just let him go."

"Why?"

"Because he will go straight to Cragen. He will tell him we got loose."

"Hmm," Rylie thinks long and hard. He releases the assistant and throws the key at him. "Let her down."

The boyish assistant obeys.

"Does Cragen have any more vials of the enhanced morus?" I ask the boy as I rub my tender wrists.

"Answer her," Rylie prompts.

The boy flinches – Rylie has never been this daunting before – and stutters a response.

"Y-yes," he says. "He has a small vial on him and left one here with me." The assistant holds up a familiar vial that trembles in his fingers. Rylie snatches it and, without much thought, smashes the vial on the floor. The boy recoils with the shatter.

"Now what?" I ask.

"We need to get to the others," Rylie states.

"And stop Cragen before he can test that other vial. But what do we do with *him*?"

"We could lock him in the closet."

I cringe. "I wouldn't if I were you."

"Then where else are we going to put him?"

I point up at my shackles. "Maybe he should just hang out for a bit?"

224

****

"Where are we?"

"A house, but I don't know where."

Rylie creaks the basement door open, pokes his head around, then steps out. I'm half tempted to turn around and remove Jacklyn's body from the basement closet. It doesn't feel right to leave her here, even though she's gone. How will Cragen dispose of the body if I leave her behind? Or will he just leave her there to rot? And what about Barris? Did he just leave him behind? Should I go find him, give him and Jacklyn the proper burial they both deserve? Do I even have the time? Who's to say the infected haven't gotten to Barris' body already, if Cragen hasn't disposed of him?

I shake my head and rapidly blink the thoughts back. I can't think about them yet. Not now. We have to get out of here. We have to help the others. I have to find Scott and Emmett and Kade and *Dylan*.

I follow Rylie, blinking against the harsh brightness of the room. The walls appear to be freshly painted the sharpest white possible, pictures offering a jarring contrast. Why would Cragen go to the trouble of repainting the interior for his makeshift compound? Unless it's not meant to serve as just a compound.

"This is Cragen's home, isn't it?" I whisper as we move along.

"You tell me." Rylie stops to point at a picture of Cragen proudly displaying his degree accreditation beside his parents, Cym and Magna. I wonder if I've ever been in this house before now, and if so, under what circumstances. But the thought is fleeting.

We do a brief sweep of the house. I'm honestly surprised by its small and homey appeal. No one inside, though we spot two mongrils outside the living room window. They guard the front stoop – I wouldn't call it guarding though. They're just lounging around on the last step with their bows slung lazily across the rail.

I pull Rylie from the window's view.

"What now?" he asks.

"Cragen hinted to me that Dylan's being held captive next door. Is that where he had you, too?"

"I-I don't know," he sputters. "It was dark and cramped. When the door opened, they threw a gunnysack over my head. You know the rest."

I groan, agitation spiking up my back. I knead my neck with my fingers.

"Great. We don't know how many mongrils are next door."

"Guess we'll have to wing it." Rylie dashes to the kitchen. He returns, sporting a rolling pin and a single-serve cast-iron frying pan. "He must have removed all the sharp utensils. Smart."

I roll my eyes and snatch the rolling pin.

We sneak out the back door. I motion for Rylie to go around the left side of the house as I dash to the right. Peaking around the corner, I note the relaxed stances of both mongrils. One still sits on the step while the man closest to me sunbathes in the grass, eyes closed, arms draped behind his head. The rolling pin splinters my thumb as I grip it tight, tiptoe forward…

But Rylie jumps out at the seated mongril and hits him. The force of his blow makes an audible crack shatter down the man's back before he hits the ground cold.

The commotion stirs the sunbather.

I lunge, slightly quicker than the jostled mongril, and he falls beside his friend. Quick scan of the area. No one.

There are two houses next to Cragen's, both more rundown-looking than his. The one on the right is a one-story home that's browned with age while the left is a rickety Victorian with broken windows. The Victorian's lawn bares charred patches toward the sidewalk.

"I'll take this one," I point to the left. "You check that one."

"No way," Rylie scoffs. He folds his arms and give a frustrated headshake. "After what just happened? Where you go, I go."

Just like his brother.

We snatch the bows and quivers from the rail before venturing forward. The inside of the Victorian doesn't look as shabby as the exterior. However, a thick layer of dust covers every inch of furniture. No sign of any mongrils on the first floor.

But someone is *definitely* on the floor above us. We stand at the base of the steps for a long moment and listen. Two people. At least, only two that I know of. Labored breathing from one as the other sneers, muffled words dripping with disdain. I recognize the sneers immediately.

I motion for Rylie to follow me up the steps. It's significantly easier to tip-toe now. *Is it the newly enhanced morus cells?* I wonder. Rylie seems to have no trouble, either, as he makes no noise on the clearly old and warn stairs. Does this confirm my theory, or are we both just stealthy creatures at heart? If only we had a friend here as a control…

Two of the doors on the second landing stand wide open. The sneering voice emanates from behind the third door. We listen and wait.

"You know, the screaming stopped forever ago," Blairs voice jeers. "I wonder how they're doing over there."

Strong breathing, but no reply.

"Bet she finally got what she deserved."

Grunts. Breathing. No reply.

As if Rylie hasn't already been spontaneously foolish enough already, he barges into the room with a loaded bow. I bring up his flank, mutely cursing him.

"Ugh. Speak of the devil." Blair swings her Rambo-like blade with dramatic hand motions. She stands beside a wooden chair, the person's back to us, hands and feet held in monster zip ties to the chair. *Dylan.* Unconscious, or just weak? Undoubtably injured by evidence of his pained breaths and the red trickle down his arm.

"I figured you'd still be…hanging out," Blair continues with a chuckle.

"Step away," Rylie interrupts.

"And if I don't?"

"I'll shoot you."

She laughs.

"Drop the knife, Blair," I say.

To our surprise, she does as I say.

"Kick it this way," I say.

She scoots the knife with her boot. Rylie steps closer, arrow only a few inches from her face, as I pick up the knife and cut Dylan free. Dylan ragdolls to the floor and grunts.

"You really think you can stop him?" Blair teases.

"We can try."

I pull Dylan to the corner of the room, prop him against the wall, and join Rylie as he backs Blair into the chair. Blair looks at me, eyes pleading, but not for mercy. As I watch her, the purple and grey veins against her sclerae become more evident. She cocks her head to the side and bats her eyelashes.

"Did Cragen get what he wanted?"

I don't answer, but she doesn't miss the clench of my jaw. Her bandage crinkles as she gives a wicked grin.

"And you're going to try to take it from him?"

"We *will* take it from him," Rylie growls next to me.

Blair laughs, this time sharper and forced. It's clear we won't get any information from her, not like this. Not with Rylie testing out his newly found boldness. I grant him a warning glance before kneeling in front of Blair. Her gaze follows me as I kneel, her grin slipping just a slight, brows furrowed.

"What did he do to you?" I ask in the smallest voice I can manage.

She leans forward and exhales, her breath hot and sour. Her dark eyes seem to blacken as her expression turns grave.

"I was dying alone," she tells me. "Those cowards were going to put me down like a dog. Cragen *saved* me. He *saved* all of us. And he needs *you* to make us stronger, to make sure no one ever needs saved again."

"But you're not saved," I try to counter. I place a hand on her knee. She shakes it off. "You're dying, Blair. Just like me. Just like *him*."

"You're lying," she spits on my shirt. But her eyes flicker with doubt.

I stand with a sigh.

Rylie straightens his bow at her again.

I clear my throat. "Cragen said he had places to go, people to see. Where is he heading?"

"Where do you think?" Blair rolls her eyes, as if it's painfully obvious.

"The community?"

"Not *your* community," she says, "though he will get to the rest of them in due time."

"Then where?"

"My old community. Dinky little town in Iowa. Those jerks are finally going to get what they deserve. And I believe you have an old friend there. Not that you'd remember her."

Rylie and I exchange a worried look.

"Why are you being so compliant?" Rylie demands, and shoves the arrow closer to her scarring face.

She laughs, hands raised.

"Can't you see this is all part of his plan?"

The laughing finally does it. I knock her out with my fist.

Dylan stirs in the corner.

"I'll take care of this one," I say. "Check on your brother."

Chapter 20

After tearing part of Blair's shirt, I successfully fashion restraints from the cloth and push her and her semi-permanent thrown into a closet. Rylie approves with a loud *Ha!* before breaking off the outside handle. She won't be following us anytime soon.

With Rylie's newly found strength, he's able to carry his brother far enough away from the two homes. We walk about a mile before he complains about the lactic acid build-up in his arms. We find another house on Elm Street of – well, wherever the hell we are – and decide to take a breather until Dylan can make the journey.

I have to clear the house of two infected, but that takes roughly two minutes. We place Dylan in a bedroom and dispose of the bodies in the backyard. Rylie joins his brother in the upstairs bedroom while I search the house for necessities.

Two cans of peaches, a can of green beans, a can of tuna, three cans of carrots, a can opener, a shotgun with ten rounds in the basement gun safe, a baseball bat, and a pair of wireless clippers. Miraculously, the clipper batteries still have some juice.

With my bounty slung in a duffle bag I found in the mudroom, I set up camp in the living area. Don't get me wrong, I'd love to be up there with the boys when Dylan wakes up, but my head feels like it might explode from pressure if I don't sit down and sort out the recent events.

It doesn't take long to do. I've always been good at suppressing unpleasant matters. Though, truthfully, this tops all the rest. After a few moments of rocking with my head between my knees and some insanely heavy breathing, I manage to pull it together – well, somewhat. Even after I'm calm, I still get flashes of Barris or Jacklyn in the back of my mind.

I want to hit something. I want to hit myself for letting this happen. I want to bash in Cragen's brains. But where would that leave me? What good would it do? The bloodshed has not proven helpful, and I know we can't counter it with *more* bloodshed. I know I'll have to live with this guilt for however long I have left. So long as Cragen isn't a threat, I think I may be able to manage that. It's only a couple of years, after all.

My neck twinges. Electricity shoots down my spine and back up a couple inches past my hairline. The sting intensifies for half a second. I coil into the couch, hugging my knees until the sting subsides.

Once I'm able to move, I dash to the bathroom and pull my collar down.

The mark is thick and black now. It takes up the center of my back and has worked its way up close to the crowning of my head. It's hard to tell, though, as my hair is too thick to properly see.

How am I supposed to keep track of this thing if I can't see it?

But I'm pulled out of my mind when an all-too familiar voice from above me exclaims "Thank god you're okay, bro!"

I run upstairs to find Dylan and Rylie locked in a brotherly embrace.

Dylan's eyes flash to me. He heaves a sigh. "Kaiya! Thank god." He spots the red splotches on my clothes and hurries over to me in the doorway, worry plastered between his brows. "Are you alright?"

No, I want to tell him. I have been tortured and experimented on, again. So no, I am not okay. And neither is your brother. We are going to be fucked up for however long we have left.

My eyes burn as I remember the cold metal scraping my muscle, my blood surging to the surface, running down to puddle at my feet...

I don't answer. He examines me for a minute. He shoulders relax when he can't find any wounds.

"I'm okay. I'm fine." It doesn't sound convincing.

"Are you sure? Is that your blood? I heard you screaming and thought something terrible happened to you. Are you hurt?"

Me? What about Rylie? I look pointedly at his brother, but his clothes aren't bloodied like mine. He must have raided the upstairs rooms and found a change of clothes.

Rylie shakes his head slightly at me. I clear my throat.

"It's a long story. I'll explain later, but I promise I'm okay. Or I will be."

Dylan smiles and pulls me into his arms. "Thank god for that." He squeezes me hard. I lean into him, the clenching in my chest vaguely subsides.

Rylie clears his throat. "Where are the others?"

"I don't know," Dylan says, pulling away. "I remember the mongrils rushing in when Nolan knocked out Cragen, and I saw the others through the window. They were running into the trees. I woke up alone in that chair. I have no clue if they even got away. Did you overhear anything?"

"Cragen was more interested in the two of us than anything," Rylie says scornfully as he moves to stand beside his brother.

More me than you, I think with a shiver. I can still feel where his lips had met my cheek.

"Are you okay?" Dylan asks.

"Fine, fine," I say. "Just a memory."

"I overheard him say something weird while I was…resting," Rylie says. Dylan shoots him a confused look, but Rylie ignores it.

"He said he had things to do, people to see, and that he'd be seeing us again soon. And then he…well, I'll just say he left."

"Do you think he meant the others?"

"I don't think so." *Places to go, people to see.* And then he had winked at me, like I was supposed to know what he meant. "Blair said there was another community, specifically the one she is from. She made it sound like Cragen was going there specifically to test the enhanced cells on someone from my past."

"Wait, *enhanced* cells?"

"I'll explain later," I wave it off. "But think about it. That's why he hasn't killed me yet. He needs more

234

test subjects before he can take and create more morus cells."

"The important thing is that he's not going after our community," Rylie says.

"No, but I bet that's where our friends went when they escaped."

"They're probably half-way home by now," Dylan says. "And they'll be safer there."

"But what about the other community?" I ask. "We only know it's in a small town in Iowa. We don't know how to get there. And Cragen's already gotten a head-start. We have to find a way to stop him!"

"We know the mongrils, and we've tracked them before," Rylie points out. "If we can pick up on their trail, maybe we can track them."

"We don't need to," Dylan says glumly. "Yuna knows the Iowa community. Her brother used to go there to get away from her. She could take us there, but it might be a lengthy journey."

"We can handle it," Rylie says with a smug grin. He withdraws a folded town map from his pocket. He sprawls it on the bedspread. "Found this one of the bedrooms, and the previous owner was even nice enough to mark it for us," he points to the red circle marked on the corner of Elm Street. "The town we are in is only a day's walk from the community. We can get a car from home, grab Yuna and some backup, and go from there."

"Okay, and if we run into the mongrils first?" I ask. "There are three of us. I can stop Cragen, but I doubt I can take on all his mongrils, too."

"We'll avoid them," Dylan assures with a hand on my shoulder.

"Let's go," Rylie urges, moving for the door. "We can come up with a plan along the way."

****

We don't get very far before we have to stop to eat. I can't remember the last time I'd had a meal. Though the cans of food I'd found earlier don't sound particularly appetizing, we scarf down three cans.

"How long was I locked down there?" I ask the guys.

"I'm not sure," Rylie answers first. "I felt like I was in that closet for several days."

"You were locked in a closet?" Dylan shakes his head. "It was only two nights. Two excruciatingly long nights."

"No kidding," I mutter, tossing my empty peach can to the side. "I would rather have been in the closet."

Dylan sets his can down and leans forward to look at me, arms resting on his knees. "What happened to you?" His voice is soft.

I don't answer, counting shotgun shells to keep myself busy. Dylan thankfully doesn't push the matter any further.

The sun has set. It's nearly dark. Rylie offers me a spoonful of green beans, which I graciously accept. Dylan doesn't eat much.

When we start walking again, Rylie leads the way. I wish I'd thought to look for a flashlight. But as we strain to see under the stars, Rylie's veins seem to sick out harshly against his skin. I look down at my own wrists. Mine are also subtly dark and radiant. I doubt Dylan will be able to see it. His eyes don't seem to be as strong as ours as he continuously trips through the dark streets.

I wonder if Rylie will tell his brother about what Cragen did. How will Dylan react, knowing his brother medically died, and that he was an experiment? No longer mundane. No longer able to carry on his blood line without further morus cell contamination. And soon, the cells will attack his body and mind just as they have Cragen's, lest Rylie be exposed to some deadly sickness soon. My eyes burn for him. Rylie's too young. He may suffer the same fate as Cragen, as the mongrils, as me. His life has been decided for him...all because he's loosely associated with me now.

"What are you thinking?" Dylan whispers. I forgot he was beside me.

"Nothing," I hedge, stepping over a pothole in the street.

But of course, I'm thinking about everything all at once. About Rylie, about what Cragen did to me, about the last two nightmares I had, about my mark and the impending end it symbolizes, and about Jacklyn and Barris. Always thinking about those two.

But what did those nightmares mean? In both instances, Dylan didn't die before I woke up. He survived. Does this mean that I finally did something right? Has Dylan's death sentence been lifted? And the less concerning question: why did Dylan leave me behind in my last dream? What does this mean? What does *any* of this mean?

"It's getting too dark," Rylie announces. "And I hear infected ahead. We should probably find a place to stop for the night."

So, we follow a dirt path off the main road until we reach an old ranch. We stay in a barn for the remainder of the night. All three of us are exhausted. More likely traumatized than exhausted.

But I can't let myself rest. Dylan and Rylie lay in the loft, sleeping on piles of hay. I listen to their soft snores and stare out the barn doors at the stars. Brilliant heavenly lights gaze down at the tops of the trees on this chilly night; the perfect romantic setting if it weren't for the walking corpses and the psychotic men hunting for more guinea pigs.

How twisted the world has become. If only we could live in a world where romance is still practiced, and extramundane violence is something that only happens in movies and video games. To think that if the experiments had never happened, I could have a family. I could have a career. I could have a significant other. Maybe even children. We could laugh and play in the backyard, take family trips…and I could take them to see my parents and siblings on the weekends. I could have my husband hold my hand as I go through chemotherapy and live every day as if it were my last.

But instead, I am here, fighting for every day because it *could* be my last.

Someone stirs in the loft. I try to enjoy the view as long as I can, but I'm eventually interrupted by a voice.

"You better get some sleep," Dylan says. "I'll take watch."

"I don't think I even can."

Dylan sits beside me, runs a hand through his already tousled hair, and asks, "What happened to you? What did Cragen do?"

"You mean besides killing my best friend?" I snap.

Dylan stays silent.

I sigh. "I'm sorry. It's been a rough couple of days. Let's leave it at that. If it weren't for me, Barris and Jacklyn would still be here."

"Stop that."

"Stop what? Telling the truth?"

"Stop feeling guilty. Stop blaming yourself."

"I can't. Because it *is* my fault. And if you were smart, you would stay away from me, or you might be next."

"Kaiya –"

"No, I'm serious. You should stay away. I should go off on my own to find Cragen. I don't want to risk anyone else. I've destroyed enough lives in the last week. I'm not going to be the reason anyone else dies."

"You really think I would just let you go at this alone?"

You did in my dream.

"We are in this together," he continues.

"But –"

"No 'but's, Kaiya," Dylan puts a friendly hand on my shoulder. "If you leave, Cragen will find you. He and the mongrils will overpower you. He will take you and drain your blood, and then there will be no hope for the rest of us. Is that really something you want to risk?"

"Well…no…" I stammer, preparing an argument in my head. "But –"

"No 'but's! We are in this together," he repeats. His eyes are heavy with sleep and grief. "We know what we signed on for. You can't carry this burden alone. Let us help you. And we will end this. *Together.*"

I groan and fall backwards to sprawl out on the floor. "I don't like this."

"No one said you had to like it. Just accept it."

"Sure, sure," I grumble. "If it keeps you all safe."

I gaze at the wooden support beams overhead. Some of the wood is rotted in the center of the beam directly above me, drooping ever so slightly towards earth. I imagine it to be like a balancing act one would see at the circus before all this, only if anyone dared to walk on it, the lumber would collapse. The beam would split in two halves with sharp fragments at the newly defined ends. The person atop would fall, legs flailing with splinters scattered in the open air. A fall like that would likely kill someone.

I realize as Dylan lays back beside me that I *am* the rotted beam. I'm wasting away. A rapidly ticking time bomb. And the person balancing atop…that's my friends. Dylan, Scott, Emmett, Rylie, Kade…all of them. And they're all doomed because of me. Because I'm rotten. Because I am doomed, too.

But I also realize in this instant just how different their perspectives of me are from my own. They're depending on me. I have to keep it together for them. I have to end this so no one else has their future stripped from them the way mine has been taken from me, the way Rylie's has been taken from him.

Dylan takes my hand in his. I don't have to look over to feel his caramel-coffee eyes focused on me. "You know you can't get rid of us that easily, right?"

I smile, still looking up. In fleeting moments like this, I'm thankful for the endless tormented dreams that have brought him to me. I can sporadically feel like a whole person again, even if just for a short while longer. Everything's a little more tolerable, like the brown of his eyes is where the earth and sun collide and being on this soil suddenly makes sense.

"I hope so."

"Better know so."

About The Author

Lora K. Kroush is a writer, editor, and mother. She was born and raised in Hamilton, Missouri and has a bachelor's degree in English with a concentration in creative writing and publishing. Lora has a husband, Cody, and two daughters, Lily and Violet.

She has experience in positions such as graphic design, marketing coordination, and editorial leadership roles from the literary and arts journals *The Mochila Review* and *Reach*.

Lora writes poetry, science fiction and romance. She has a poetry book out titled *Scarred Wonderland* and a novel titled *Recurrence*, both published by *Amazing Things Press*. She continues to work on *The Morus Series* along with three other novel-sized projects. In her free time, she enjoys watching horror films and spoiling her daughters.

Acknowledgements

A special thank you to my family and friends for always showering me with support and love. To the educators who have nurtured my love for writing, I will always be grateful.

Check out these books from

Amazing Things Press

Keeper of the Mountain by Nshan Erganian

Rare Blood Sect by Robert L. Justus

Survival In the Kitchen by Sharon Boyle

Stop Beating the Dead Horse by Julie L. Casey

In Daddy's Hands by Julie L. Casey

MariKay's Rainbow by Marilyn Weimer

Seeking the Green Flash by Lanny Daise

Thought Control by Robert L. Justus

Fun Activities to Help Little Ones Talk by

Kathy Blair

Bighorn by James Ozenberger

Post Exodus by Robert Christiansen

Rawnie's Mirage by Marilyn Weimer

All American Prizefighter by Rob Calloway

Fall of Grace by Rachel Riley and Sharon Spiegel

Taming the Whirlwind by Lindsey Heidle

John Henry's War by Larry W. Anderson

The Brothers' Murder by Brenda Grant

A Good Life by Sarah Rowan

The Thornless Rose: Fire Blush by Samantha Fidler-Newby

Made in USA - Crawfordsville, IN
18525_9781949830644
03.01.2022 1329